The Last Electric House

Peter Ullian

SWAMP ANGEL PRESS

PETER ULLIAN

ISBN: 978-0-578-60189-2

DEDICATION

To my departed mentors, Harold Prince and Ed Gorman, for their inspiration.

To everyone striving to avert the cataclysm we are creating for ourselves.

To my wife and children, for everything.

Table of Contents

Chapter One...3

Chapter Two..8

Chapter Three 12

Chapter Four...16

Chapter Five 22

Chapter Six..26

Chapter Seven..30

Chapter Eight..31

Chapter Nine 35

Chapter Ten 39

Chapter Eleven...41

Chapter Twelve 43

Chapter Thirteen......................................45

Chapter Fourteen 47

Chapter Fifteen...49

Chapter Sixteen 51

Chapter Seventeen 54

Chapter Eighteen 56

Chapter Nineteen 58

Chapter Twenty...63

Chapter Twenty-One 65

Chapter Twenty-Two 67

Chapter Twenty-Three..............................71

Chapter Twenty-Four 74

Chapter Twenty-Five 77

Chapter Twenty-Six.. 79

Chapter Twenty-Seven 82

Chapter Twenty-Eight 84

Chapter Twenty-Nine 89

Chapter Thirty 91

Chapter Thirty-One 92

Chapter Thirty-Two 97

Chapter Thirty-Three 99

Chapter Thirty-Four 102

Chapter Thirty-Five 104

Chapter Thirty-Six 106

Chapter Thirty-Seven 108

Chapter Thirty-Eight... 110

Chapter Thirty-Nine 112

Chapter Forty 114

Chapter Forty-One 117

Chapter Forty-Two 120

Chapter Forty-Three 122

Chapter Forty-Four 125

Chapter Forty-Five.. 127

Chapter Forty-Six 130

Chapter Forty-Seven 133

Chapter Forty-Eight 135

Chapter Forty-Nine 137

Chapter Fifty 139

Chapter Fifty-One 142

Chapter Fifty-Two 146

Chapter Fifty-Three...148

Chapter Fifty-Four 149

Chapter Fifty-Five 151

Chapter Fifty-Six...153

Chapter Fifty-Seven 156

Chapter Fifty-Eight 158

Chapter Fifty-Nine 161

Chapter Sixty..166

Chapter Sixty-One..169

Chapter Sixty-Two..171

Chapter Sixty-Three 172

Chapter Sixty-Four...175

Chapter Sixty-Five 180

Chapter Sixty-Six...183

Chapter Sixty-Seven 186

Chapter Sixty-Eight..188

Chapter Sixty-Nine 192

Chapter Seventy..197

Chapter Seventy-One 203

Chapter Seventy-Two 206

Chapter Seventy-Three.....................................208

AUTHOR'S NOTE

When I began this book, not that long ago, the future
imagined in its pages seemed far off.

Today, only a few years later, it seems much closer at hand.

I still hope we are brave enough to imagine a better one.

Chapter One

Kim took a time out from the death-watch for her father to contemplate the end of the world, and consider next steps.

She sat on the back gallery of her family's 19th century home, and looked out at the valley, shimmering in the gloaming. Here and there, she could see the dim light of a candle or two in a window of a far-off neighbor's farmhouse, small bulwarks against the coming dark. The house she shared with her sister, Ingrid, and their ailing father was the only house in the valley outfitted with solar panels, and so the only house with electricity, now that there wasn't enough diesel or propane left to run anyone's generators. They could light their house up like a beacon to be seen atop their property from miles around. But Kim took care not to do that. She didn't want to rub their good fortune in her neighbors' faces. She already worried her family had never been particularly well-liked in the valley. She was afraid if they weren't sensitive about their electricity use, dislike would turn to hatred. Accordingly, all the lights in the house were off, except for the bedside lamp in her father's room, where Ingrid, her sister, now sat vigil, waiting for the end.

Ingrid was not so sensitive about electricity usage. Kim could hear her now, marching down the stairs, accompanied by the sound of light switches flicking. Steadily, the light on the gallery grew brighter as the light from inside spilled through the windows and open door.

Kim waited for her sister. With the coming evening, the air began to cool, marginally, but the humidity remained. Every breath, thought Kim, felt like sucking a raincloud into her lungs. Already, her shirt was soaking through with perspiration.

Once their father was gone, Kim wondered, how would they make their way in this world, when there might be no more world to speak of beyond the valley in which they lived? Ingrid hadn't even finished college before everything fell apart; Kim was just a few years out. They were still young, they had their whole lives ahead of them -- but what were they to do with it? Before the collapse, they had imagined their world was vast and unlimited; now, it was restricted to this valley, this community, where they had been raised, and which they had always assumed they would one day leave behind.

Ingrid stood in the doorway. Her eyes looked distracted, distant; Kim figured she was probably stoned. She usually was. Even so, she looked beautiful, Kim thought. Ingrid almost always looked beautiful. Kim resented her little sister for always looking so effortlessly beautiful.

"What did I tell you about turning on all the lights?" Kim scolded.

"I think Dad's dying," Ingrid said.

Kim sighed. "Dad's been dying for months," she said.

"No, I mean, I think he's really dying," Ingrid said. "I mean, like, *now*."

Kim looked at her sister. She could tell she was serious.

Harper, the Sheriff, was on her way to one of the two checkpoints leading out of the valley, when she pulled her Crown Vic over to the side of the street because her passage was blocked by a small crowd watching two men trying to punch each other into submission outside the Silver Dollar Saloon.

One of the men she recognized as Ebert Rollings, who worked for Henry Lowry. Lowry had formerly been one of the most powerful men in the valley, before the collapse. The other man, she didn't recognize. Both men were bare-chested and fighting bare-knuckled. Someone was going to get seriously hurt.

The crowd shouted and cheered on the men, placing bets, it appeared. Harper wasn't quite sure what they were using to wager, as currency was just so much paper since the collapse.

Harper saw Henry Lowry in the crowd and went up to him. "This your event, Henry?"

Lowry smiled a smile Harper found utterly insincere. "People need some entertainment," he said. "Now that the TV and internet are gone forever, and there's no more movies."

Ebert threw a punch that connected with the other man, a large fellow with stringy black hair. The blow hit the man on the mouth and knocked him back several steps. He wobbled on his feet and spat a gob of bloody phlegm. But he did not go down.

"Ever tried reading a book, Henry?" Harper asked. "Or having a sing-along? I bet some of your crew can play instruments."

The man with the stringy black hair threw a punch and connected with the side of Ebert's head. Ebert staggered, shaking his head to regain his equilibrium.

"You gonna stop this, or am I?" Harper asked Lowry.

Lowry looked at her skeptically. "You think you can stop this on your own?"

Harper put her hand on the butt of her sidearm. "You want me to?"

Lowry looked at her for what felt like a long time, regarding her, trying to take her measure. He was a man used to being in charge, and not having his authority questioned.

Then he raised a hand and shouted, "All right, gentlemen! That'll do. We'll call it a draw."

Immediately, the men stopped fighting.

"You've got 'em well trained," Harper said. "Let's try to keep the streets free of human cock fighting, Ok, Henry? As far as we know, this valley is the last bastion of civilization since the collapse. Let's keep it that way."

As Harper made her way back to the Crown Vic, Lacey Rollings, Ebert's wife, approached her. "How's your girlfriends up on the hill?" she asked.

"You mean Kim and Ingrid?" Harper said. "Still waiting

for their daddy to die."

"Tragic as that sounds, it must be nice waiting for him to die with air conditioning and electric power," Lacy said. "While the rest of us got nothing."

"The Emergency Council is meeting soon to look at how resources in the valley are distributed," Harper said. "Everyone is going to do their part."

"Including your girlfriends?"

"Including them. Including me. Including you. Including Henry Lowry." She nodded towards Lowry, who was drinking whiskey with the two bloodied combatants, handing them beveled glasses and pouring from a bottle of Jack Daniels, a precious and rare commodity since the end of the world as they knew it.

"Like to see you make that happen," Lacey said.

"It'll happen," Harper said, getting into the Crown Vic, and wondering how she was going to make it happen.

Ingrid and Kim sat at their father's bedside as he slowly died. They listened to his breathing grow more shallow and labored throughout the night.

"What are we going to do once he's gone?" Ingrid asked.

"I don't know," Kim admitted. "Try to keep going, I guess."

"Should we find boyfriends?" Ingrid said.

Kim scowled at her. "Is that all you think about?"

Ingrid pouted. "Well, you said we should keep going," she replied. "It's the end of the world as we know it. Why can't we have boyfriends?"

Kim sighed, and tried not to imagine the continued effort it would take to look after her sister until the day Ingrid finally, if ever, grew the fuck up.

At the checkpoint, Harper met with Dawkins, one of her most experienced deputies, and Percy, one of her least. It was dark by now, and the road that ran from the checkpoint out beyond the valley was pitch black, and felt ominous to Harper, filled with the unknown.

"What's the report, gentlemen?" Harper said.

"You know how the refugees coming from outside the valley had slowed to a trickle, lately, and then stopped altogether?" Dawkins said. "Well, young Percy here went about three miles out to reconnoiter."

Harper gave Percy a look to make her displeasure plain. "Why the hell did you do that?" she said. "I can't afford to lose a single deputy to some dumb adventure."

Percy looked down, sheepishly. "I just thought I'd go see what I could see," he said.

Harper sighed. "What did you see?"

Percy looked up and reported eagerly. "I saw people's things. Clothes. Duffels. Backpacks. A bicycle. Stuff that looked like it had been rifled through, some stuff scattered. Maybe some stuff taken, hard to tell. No people, though. No live ones, I mean. I saw a body. Mostly just bones and some dried-out flesh, looked like jerky. Buzzards had been over him good. What's that mean, you think, Sheriff?"

Harper knew exactly what that meant. "People are still trying to make it to our valley," she said. "At least some of them are. But someone else is waiting for them before they get here."

Dawkins screwed up his face with worry. "What're we going to do about it?" he said.

"Make sure whoever's waiting for them doesn't get into the valley," Harper said. "Let's double the deputies at the checkpoints."

"What do we do about those poor people getting intercepted?" Percy asked.

"Not much we can do," Harper said. She was not going to risk the lives of her deputies to rescue refugees three miles or more outside the valley. "We can pray for them, I guess."

Chapter Two

Their father stopped breathing.

Kim and Ingrid sat there, silently. Waiting. Listening. Wondering if their father would take another breath, or, if this time, he was really done.

Kim realized she had been holding her own breath. She let it out, slowly.

"I think he's really gone now," Kim said.

They sat for a long time, trying to come to terms with it. To neither one of them did their father's passing seem quite real. To Kim, after nursing her father through his final months, it seemed impossible to comprehend that he was actually gone. For Ingrid, she was too stoned to fully absorb the impact of what had happened.

"So," Ingrid said, dreamily. "What do we do now? I don't mean existentially. I mean, practically. How do we deal with dead bodies after the end of the world?"

It was a good question and Kim, who liked to think of herself as the responsible one, the one with a head on her shoulders, was surprised to discover she didn't know the answer. Her sister, Ingrid, was the one who never thought ahead, who never considered consequences. Kim always did. Yet, until this moment, she had never considered what to do after the inevitable finally arrived. She realized that, on some level, she had been in denial – she had understood, intellectually, her father was dying; but emotionally, she refused to believe it. She had resigned herself to a lifetime of bedpans and sponge baths, but had not seriously considered a lifetime of absence.

Kim tried to think things over. Emotions whirled inside her, but they were confused, and felt far away. Grief and relief were trying to elbow one another out of the way, making it impossible for her to fully experience either one. Mostly, she felt exhausted, and empty.

The local funeral home was still in business, although they undoubtedly lacked the chemicals they had used in the past to embalm. Kim wasn't sure how they were doing on coffins. She had no idea if the coffins they used in the past were locally manufactured or ordered from afar. There were plenty of trees in the mountains around the valley, so it was possible they were just banging together simple wooden caskets. Or maybe they were even burying people in the ground wrapped in a shroud, or a sheet. Kim knew, of course, people had died since everything collapsed – plenty of people -- but Kim hadn't attended any of the funerals. She'd been too busy tending to her father, and, besides, there were few people in the valley with whom her family had been close enough to warrant attending a funeral.

She decided, in the spirit of her father's life, they would handle things themselves. He had often expressed his desire that there be no funeral to honor him. Instead, he wanted a big party, with everybody welcome. Then he wanted his body fed to their pigs.

Kim wasn't sure about that last part. She had to consider exactly how that would work.

They couldn't just let his corpse sit around, however. Not with this heat – not with these days in which there were no more seasons and nothing but relentless sun during the day and oppressive humidity at night.

She figured they needed to put him in the meat locker with the ice cream, pork, venison, chickens, wild turkey, and goat.

That, she had to admit, didn't sound entirely hygienic.

"We need to wash his body," Kim said, abruptly, as the thought occurred to her.

"What?" Ingrid said, then added: "Gross."

"We need to wash him and then wrap him in a shroud."

"Where do we get a shroud?" Ingrid asked. "Do they sell them at the general store?"

"We can use a bedsheet," Kim said. "Not this one," she added, pointing to the one on which her father's body lay. "A fresh one."

Ingrid looked at her hazily. "I'll get one," she said, and left the room.

Kim heard her walking down the stairs and out the back door, presumably heading towards the freshly laundered sheets that hung on the line.

Kim looked at her father. The sunken cheeks, the aquiline nose, once so grand and handsome, now looking so out of place on the lifeless face, poleaxed her. It was inconceivable that a man so vital was now nothing but a flesh-bag of bones and meat.

Then again, only two years ago, if someone had told her that everything – as far as anyone could tell -- outside the valley would be wiped away, all the cities and towns and farms and universities and movie studios and publishing houses and militaries and police and governments and music companies and tech entrepreneurs and comic books and internet, everything that made up this big, vital, expansive world, all would collapse in a conflagration of flooding, wildfires, fuel shortages, droughts, grid collapse, riots, refugees, massive hurricanes, enormous tornados, burning rainforests, melting icecaps, and disease . . . she wouldn't have believed it.

And yet, that had come to pass. And, if she thought about it, she had to admit, the end of all that had seemed kind of inevitable, too, to anyone willing to look at reality without self-deception. Kim liked to think of herself as someone unafraid to look the world in the eye and meet it on its own terms, but she had to concede, even as she saw what in retrospect could only be interpreted at warning signs, she had held onto an irrational belief that disaster would ultimately be avoided.

But disaster had not been avoided.

Ingrid, stumbling into the room with a bedsheet, tore Kim from her thoughts.

"Let's use this one," Ingrid said, and held up a bedsheet covered in writing.

It took Kim a moment to register what she was looking

at. It was a bedsheet on which was printed the lyrics to a John Lennon song.

"It's your 'Imagine' bedsheet," Kim said. "You love that."

"I think Daddy would like to be buried in it," Ingrid said.

Kim had thought a solid white bedsheet would be more dignified and appropriate, but she recognized the significance of her sister's gesture and wanted to honor it.

Kim got up and went to Ingrid, taking the bedsheet from her. "This will be perfect," she said.

Ingrid's looked at her, her eyes welling with tears, her face flushing.

Kim took her in her arms and Ingrid began to weep into her shoulder, great, heaving sobs.

Kim was envious of those sobs. She wished she could allow herself to feel that intensely.

Kim's eyes welled with tears, but she did not allow herself to sob as her sister did. She did not like to cry in front of her sister. It always made her feel weak.

Chapter Three

Harper and her Uncle Stan saw what was coming before anyone else in the valley. They were only just ahead of the curve, but it was enough. Barely. For Harper, anyway. For Uncle Stan, not so much.

Uncle Stan saw it first, although he didn't say it outright. Harper only knew what he saw when she heard the sharp report of his service revolver and rushed into his office in the Sheriff's department to find the walls behind his desk painted with his blood and brain matter.

Harper, Stan's deputy as well as his niece, wanted to cry when she saw the man she loved and admired laid low by his own hand. Stan had been her favorite uncle, her mentor – the person, more than any other, whom she wanted to be when she grew up. Or, so she had thought.

She choked back her tears. Stan had done this because he knew that what was coming was what she herself feared was coming. She'd been reassuring herself it wouldn't get that bad – things would be tough, but people would pull together, and pull through. She knew now that Stan was certain it *would* get that bad, bad enough that he couldn't bear to live to see it, couldn't bear to face the helplessness he would feel as things went to shit and he could do nothing to prevent it – people would not pull together, she now knew, and they would not pull through. Not most of them, anyway.

Stan was the toughest, most resourceful man she had ever known – and she had served in Iraq and Afghanistan. If what he saw coming was too much for him to bear, then what was coming was really going to be bad. Things were on the verge of collapse, she now knew. There would be no help from outside. The things they had now in their homes and in the local stores would not be replenished. There would be no more deliveries. No more medicine. No more gasoline. No more food, other than what they could grow, or raise, or already had in their larders. There would be no federal or state authority to help, no FEMA, National Guard, no Red Cross. The electricity would go out. The phones would die. There would be no more internet.

They were on their own.

Harper knew she had three options. She could wait, and try, and probably fail, to do her job as things deteriorated. Or she could blow out her own brains so she wouldn't have to face it, as her uncle had done.

Or she could do a terrible thing that might save some of the people in the valley she was sworn to protect.

Harper chose the third option, and by that evening, she'd organized the Sheriff's department and every citizen in the county with a gun, pick up, or semi to help. More than a few long-haul truckers lived in the valley, and she also had the foresight to commandeer the local school busses, as well as the trucks that transported timber, livestock, and crops.

The power grid went down just as they headed out of the valley.

By morning they returned -- most of them. They'd encountered little resistance. People were too confused, scared, and disorganized to resist. The state police were all in the major cities dealing with the riots and the looting. The National Guard had also been deployed to the cities, leaving their armories barely manned and easily overwhelmed. Local law enforcement was out-gunned. Many of them had already deserted their posts.

Five men and two pick-up trucks didn't return. Harper never found out what happened to them.

It didn't much matter, not in the big picture, anyway. A convoy of trucks and cars and pick-ups packed with everything they could acquire and steal, stuffed with every non-perishable item from every big box store, gun shop, pharmacy, grocery store, hospital, and granary within a thirty-mile radius rolled into the valley that morning. They had loaded up on dry goods, seeds, ammunition, gasoline, canned goods, kerosene, diesel, propane, toiletries, medicine, tools, textiles, cloth, clothing, shoes, guns -- including two fifty caliber weapons nicked from the National Guard armory -- and anything else they could carry. Harper commandeered the high school gymnasium for storage, and organized a team to sort, and guard, the contraband.

This was why, not long thereafter when things really went to shit, the valley had managed to avoid the worst of it. This was why, while those outside the valley starved, those within the valley ate, if not well, then at least adequately. This was why, when shortages crippled central authority and emergency response outside the valley, Harper and her deputies had managed, barely, to maintain order. This was why, when the myriad of diseases released by the melting permafrost up north and the sweltering tropics down south made their way to the valley, the death rate in the county was a fraction of what it had been everywhere else.

Harper often wondered what the tipping point for her uncle had been. Was it when the seawalls gave way and flooded the eastern seaboard? Or when California went dark? Or the news of the almost complete crop failures in the drought-stricken Midwest? Or that there was no more fuel coming, ever, either foreign or domestic? Or when it became apparent that there was no Federal government anymore to speak of, and the state governments weren't up to the task of filling the void? Or was it the reports of rioting and refugees and pandemic in the state capitol and beyond?

Harper didn't know. She'd helped give the valley a fighting chance. But at night, she lay awake thinking about those people outside the valley who never had one – some of them, in part, because of her.

Some of those very people wandered into the valley, a trickle of refugees – far fewer than she expected. Most didn't make it that far. Some probably died on the road, from exhaustion, starvation, disease, or marauders. For others, by the time they realized they had to flee their homes, it was too late.

Harper made sure those who made it to the valley were vetted. She interviewed each one, personally. She had Doc Wilson check them out. If she thought they were ok, and if the Doc thought they were healthy, she made sure they were put up with a local family.

If they felt wrong, she sent them back out on the open road.

The ones she sent away haunted her dreams at night. They were joined by the ones who never made it to the valley. Harper saw them in such vivid and specific detail that when she woke in the morning, she was convinced she had been visited by the ghosts of the dead rather than her own imagination.

Now that she knew the recent trickle of refugees were being waylaid about three miles or so from the checkpoint into the valley, that gave her imagination a whole new set of faces to haunt her at night.

Often, as she lay in bed at night wondering who would meet her in her dreams to come, she wished she had some of that good, strong whiskey her uncle kept in his desk drawer, to chase away the nightmares.

But whiskey was a finite commodity, and that bottle had been emptied long ago.

Chapter Four

It was early morning, two days later, and Ingrid's head was pounding.

She suspected there might be a troll with a hammer inside her skull, pounding in time to the blood surging with her pulse, trying to split her cranium and crawl out into the hot, fetid air and dance a jig on her aching, nerve-wracked body. Her stomach, sour and acidic, churned, and she struggled to keep down whatever was in there, as bile rose and burned her throat.

She looked around the back gallery outside her home and through the spots flashing before her eyes, saw beer and whiskey bottles and half empty glasses and even cigarette butts – who still had cigarettes? – in overflowing ashtrays. They'd had a good time on her and Kim's dime, she thought, all those people who showed up to pay their respects, if that's what you'd call it. Ingrid suspected their interest was more in the whiskey than respect. These people may have been their neighbors for their whole lives long, but Ingrid doubted they were truly their friends. A wake – or shiva, or whatever it was (that was funny, she thought for a second, a hillbilly shiva) – was always an opportunity to party down for these people.

Ingrid took a breath and felt a little remorseful. Her neighbors had all brought food – shitty food, yes, made from whatever canned goods they could scrounge and what meager, withered crops they could grow in their gardens, or skinny, gristly chickens they could raise in their yards, or stringy, gamey squirrels or raccoons they could kill with double-aught buckshot (Christ, they'd be picking pellets out of their teeth for weeks) – but still, they had used finite resources to make a gesture of goodwill to Ingrid and her sister in their grief.

She considered the food they had brought – mostly white-trash casseroles – and thought they'd have to refrigerate most of it, which was actually something they could do, since the solar panels on the roof made their childhood home one of the only still-electrified houses in the valley. Then she thought of her father, wrapped in a shroud and lying in the meat locker downstairs next to the cuts of pork and venison and tubs of ice cream, and she felt like crying.

She didn't cry, though. She tamped down the feeling along with the rising bile in her gullet and she tried to gather her thoughts for the imminent arrival of Harper, coming on behalf of the County Emergency Council – whatever exactly that was.

Ingrid found her thoughts too scattered to gather. She decided to rehearse what she wanted to say out loud, in the hope that the act of speaking would provide clarity of thinking.

"I think the thing of it is ..." she began, trailing off, imagining Harper standing there looking serious and super-cute in her Sheriff uniform. She took a breath and continued. "The multitude of . . . factors" – what kind of factors? She had to be specific. No special pleading. "I mean, mitigating factors . . . multitudinous factors of utter . . ." She couldn't think of the word. She knew there was a word, somewhere, out there, just beyond the limits of her consciousness, floating in the fog of her mind, just outside the parameter of her ability to think clearly, which, admittedly, was severely circumscribed at the moment. Unable to settle upon the word, she uttered "mitigation-osity," thinking she'd return to that moment in her remarks later on and replace it with something better. She went on. "Which, so to say . . . "Ingrid paused, questioning the direction in which these remarks were going. "Well, maybe mitigationosity is too mild," she admitted out loud to herself.

"What the fuck are you talking about?" said a voice.

Ingrid looked up and saw Kim, looking at her with

disapproval. She had no idea how long Kim had been standing there, listening to her, judging her.

Ingrid resented her big sister. Her sister always had it together. Ingrid never had it together. Here they were, moments before Harper was scheduled to arrive, and Ingrid hadn't slept, hadn't showered, smelled like swamp gas, flatulence, and BO, and her hair was a disaster. Kim was clean, neat, dressed, and ready to greet the day and whatever came with it.

"I'm thinking on my feet," Ingrid said.

"You call that thinking?"

Fuck you, Ingrid thought. "Your ass is thinking."

"You're not making any sense."

"Your ass isn't making any sense," Ingrid countered.

"Are you high?"

"Your ass is high."

Kim stared at her, her teeth gritted, her lips pressed together, her nostrils flared, her nose crinkled. Ingrid always got a kick out of it when she could get her sister to make that face.

"Yes," Ingrid admitted. "I'm high." She had pretty much been drinking and smoking doobies all night, and had just toked another doobie about fifteen minutes ago. So, yeah, she was good and high.

"Ingrid," Kim said, soberly.

"Kim," Ingrid replied, less so.

"You cannot deal with this high."

"I can't deal with this sober," Ingrid countered, she thought sensibly.

"You can't deal with it more if you're high."

"I'm so not sure that's true," Ingrid said.

"Take my word for it."

For some reason, that pissed off Ingrid a little bit. "Why should I take your word for it?" she demanded. "Who are you? What kind of expertise do you bring to the situation? No one brings any expertise to this situation. Until recently, this situation didn't exist."

"Well," Kim said, with her patented condescending

patient superiority, "I was in the Peace Corps."

Oh, there we go, Ingrid thought. The fucking Peace Corps. Always with the fucking Peace Corps. Little Miss Responsibility and her fucking Peace Corps. If it wasn't for the fucking Peace Corps, Ingrid didn't know what. Sometimes she felt as if Kim had done her stint in the Peace Corps just so she'd have something else to rub Ingrid's face in. Not like she didn't have enough already.

"Your ass was in the Peace Corps," Ingrid relied.

"*Your* ass was in the Peace Corps," Kim said.

Ingrid always enjoyed it when she managed to frustrate Kim enough to force her down to her level of childishness.

"My ass was not in the Peace Corps," Ingrid reminded her.

"No kidding."

"I am so high right now," Ingrid confessed.

"Where were you last night?" Kim said. "Did you get any sleep? You smell like lake water, farts, and dirty underwear. Go sober up or something. And if you tell my ass to go sober up, I'm going to smack you."

Ingrid spent several long moments considering how to reply.

"Your ass is going to smack me," she said at length. She was rather proud of that riposte. It didn't give Kim an excuse to smack her, but it maintained the appropriate level of disdain.

Kim glared at her for so long, Ingrid wondered if maybe she was going to smack her anyway.

"You are literally the dumbest person alive," Kim said.

"You mean figuratively," Ingrid clarified.

"No, I mean literally."

"You do not mean literally." Ingrid was a little offended at the notion that of all the dumb people in the world, she was the dumbest. "There is no way I am the dumbest person."

"All other contenders are dead. You're the dumbest person left alive."

That was a heady thought. Ingrid wondered if it was true. They hadn't heard from the world outside of the valley in months, so if things were really as bad as they suspected they were, if most of the nation – not to say the world – really had succumbed to mass casualties and food shortages and riots and drought and wildfires and floods and massive hurricanes and dust storms and mile-wide F5 tornados and unrelenting heat and incinerated rainforests and liquefied icecaps and the collapse of central authority and anarchy and disease, as they suspected – then a lot of dumb people were probably dead. A lot of smart people, too. But certainly, a lot of dumb ones. So, Ingrid supposed she did have a lot less competition in this regard.

But then Ingrid thought of her neighbors in the county who, so far, were managing to survive, and her sister's accusation made her mad. "I am not dumber than every toothless redneck in the valley," she insisted.

"You're dumber than the dumbest one of them."

"Your ass is – "

Kim interrupted. "Take a shower. Sober up."

"There's no hot water."

"Take a cold shower. Why is there no hot water?"

"The thingy is broken or something."

"What thingy?"

"The thingy that makes the hot water." Ingrid didn't know the word for the thingy but she could visualize it pretty well.

"Why didn't you fix it?"

Ingrid laughed. "I don't know how to fix it. Dad always taught you how to make things run around here, he never taught me. Besides, I am totally high."

"He taught you."

"Then how come I don't know?"

"Because when he taught you, you were totally high."

"It's not my fault Dad grew such primo herb."

"Why didn't you tell me about it?"

"The weed? I assumed you knew. It's how he put us through college and everything."

"I mean about the hot water thingy," Kim said, annoyed.

"I'm telling you now."

"Go take a cold shower. The better to sober yourself up. It's a million degrees outside, anyway, why do you want to take a hot shower?"

"Because even when it's hot and humid, a cold shower is awful."

"Drink some coffee."

"Your ass should drink some coffee."

"Go."

Ingrid stood for a moment, trying to think of one last obnoxious comment with which to annoy her sister. She stood for several moments, concentrating hard, but discovered the well had run dry.

Instead, she farted, long and loud.

It was a very satiating flatulence. It relieved a lot of stress in all sorts of ways, and Ingrid felt it served as an appropriate capstone to the conversation.

Kim stared at her, rage burning in her face, making her cheeks flush.

Satisfied, Ingrid left the room.

Ingrid staggered up the stairs, her head pounding, her stomach churning. She reached the bathroom, and immediately vomited into the toilet. She stripped off her clothes and threw them towards the hamper. They missed, and instead scattered around the floor. She knew this would annoy Kim, so she didn't bother to pick them up. She looked at herself in the full-length mirror on the door. She liked to think of herself as the prettier sister, but right now, her hair a disaster, her body flushed and stinking, she felt anything but.

Ingrid turned on the shower and waited for the water to heat up. Then she remembered it wasn't going to. She held her breath and stepped into the cold spray.

Chapter Five

Troy and Lilly were the last.

They'd left with a half dozen, traipsing out of the city at night, avoiding the riots and the burning cars, the National Guard shooting live ammunition, the smell of tear gas and gunpowder and fire following them, it seemed, for miles, stinging their eyes and choking their throats, clinging to their clothes.

When things went to shit, it had happened fast.

First the lights went out and, with it, the internet. That was weird. Everyone felt cut off. Everyone *was* cut off. The university tried to keep things going for a while, holding classes even without electricity. Everyone still thought the crisis was going to pass. But it didn't pass, it kept getting worse, by exponential degrees. Refugees kept coming -- from the coast, where communities were being levelled by flooding and massive hurricanes, and from inland, where there was drought and massive crop failures and dust storms and recurrent F5 tornados miles wide, and from out west where huge wildfires were burning up entire states. Troy don't know why they kept coming. They figured in a city, he supposed, the government would take care of them. But the government couldn't keep up with it. The Federal authorities went radio silent, and then the state, and then there was only the city government, and they didn't know what the fuck to do. They were sticking the refugees everywhere, even on campus. There wasn't enough food, and there wasn't enough water, and there was no fuel except for emergency vehicles, and the lights were out. There were riots. And looting. Every day, every night. Eventually, the university cancelled classes. But no one had any way to get home by then. There was no more transportation, and even if you had a car, the gas pumps weren't working once the power went out, and even if they had been working, or could find someone who knew how to operate them manually, they didn't have any gas in them, because there wasn't any. And because there was no gas, there were no more deliveries of food or medicine.

Then, when things really went to shit, it got real road-warrior real fast. The authorities just completely disappeared, overnight, it seemed.

Except for the bodies. The government kept picking up the bodies. Or someone did. With garbage trucks, every morning. What gas they had they seemed to use for the trucks that picked up the bodies.

There were a lot of bodies. They just kept piling up. People kept dying. No food, no water, people dying from treatable injuries or infections or illnesses because there were no more medicines, no more electricity for anesthesia for surgeries, people killing each other over a can of beans, and the bodies just lying there in the street. The hospitals tried to keep going, but once they ran out of meds, they just became a place to store sick people until they died, and then they didn't even have enough room to store the dying.

Something swept through the city and took out a lot of people. Everyone assumed it was one of the ice-age diseases they'd heard about, unfrozen from the melting permafrost in the arctic circle, which had been swiftly making their way south. Some speculated it was some kind of tropical disease finding its way north, incubated by the tropical temperatures and humidity that was now pretty much the norm in every northern clime. Some said it was probably both, a double-whammy. Antibiotics or antivirals, depending on the illness, they were told, could have saved almost everybody. But there were no more antibiotics or antivirals, and there was no more gas to fuel trucks to bring in more antibiotics or antivirals, and no one knew if anyone was even manufacturing antibiotics or antivirals anymore because there was no communication to anywhere. So, a lot of people died, and more bodies piled up.

And then they stopped picking up the bodies in the

street. One day, it just didn't happen. Then the next day. And the next. Bodies kept piling up, but the trucks had stopped coming. Maybe they were out of gas. Maybe there was no one left to drive them.

That seemed a bad omen. Troy, Lilly, Gus, Tammy, Donnie, and Roy high-tailed it out at that point. They'd held out a while, because they had enough foresight to fill up a shitload of containers with water from the tap before the taps went dry, and stocked up on a ton of canned goods. After the eastern seaboard went down, they knew enough to stock up. But by the time the trucks stopped picking up the bodies, they were running low on everything.

They left at night, taking what they could carry, which was not enough, they knew. Troy and Lilly wore their matching Johnny Cash t-shirts – the one of the Man in Black flipping the bird at the camera at San Quentin. They weren't sure why – Troy supposed Johnny's insolent rebelliousness gave them courage.

No one brought a change of clothes. What space they had in the backpacks they needed for food and water.

Lilly wore the shark-tooth pendant Troy had given her under her t-shirt. It wasn't worth much, but they didn't want anyone to mistakenly think it was. Troy carried his backpacker guitar on his shoulder, a luxury he knew they couldn't afford. Still, he thought, if they should find refuge somewhere, they would undoubtedly have to make their own entertainment if they were ever to be entertained again, and what was the point of surviving if merely surviving was all there was? There had to be something more. If there was to be no more movies, no more TV, no more internet, no more books, perhaps there could still be music.

On the guitar, Lilly had used a sharpie to print the words in impeccable calligraphy: "This Machine Surrounds Hate and Forces it to Surrender." The words were Pete Seeger's, words he had written on his banjo. They were good words. It was good to be optimistic, Lilly said.

As they set out through the city, they saw fires, burning cars, marauding people, everywhere. It took them three days to make it out of town, traveling at night, hiding during the day.

They hit the open road and hoped for the best.

Chapter Six

Kim looked around the wide gallery on the back of the house and immediately felt ashamed at the state of things. She grabbed the wastebasket and quickly dumped the ashtrays into it. She collected the dirty glasses on a tray and brought them into the kitchen. She made coffee, and went back out onto the gallery, bearing two cups. She set them on a table and collected the beer bottles, putting them in the recycling bin -- even though there was no recycling anymore, the bottles could be reused for their home-brewed beer.

As she worked, she felt the heat of the day descend on her skin as beads of sweat began to form, and her fresh and clean sundress began to stick to her body. She checked her underarms, relieved that her deodorant was holding up. She wondered what they'd do when their supplies ran out. People used to make stuff like that, she thought, before mass production. She'd have to find out how they did it. She wondered if they had a book on that kind of stuff in her dad's library. Dad had been into all that living off the grid stuff, although it was more in theory than in practice – until the grid actually had gone down, and everyone had to live off it, if they were going to live at all. At that point, it turned out to be a good thing that he'd put in solar panels and stocked up on medicine, canned goods, and other supplies. In addition, the farm – the part that didn't grow weed – was a mostly self-sufficient enterprise. They could live on their own for a long time – maybe forever.

Kim wondered if they wanted to.

Kim heard Harper's patrol car pull up on the gravel driveway, and knew she'd be coming around back to the gallery first, rather than knocking on the front door. Kim capped the half empty whiskey bottles, picked up the coffee cups, and handed one to Harper, in uniform, just as she climbed the steps to the gallery, a Model 700 Remington Rifle on her shoulder and a Smith and Wesson M&P9 standard issue sidearm on her hip.

"You're early," Kim said.

Harper took the coffee, and drank a big gulp, savoring the flavor. She rested her Remington on the gallery railing.

"God, that's good," Harper said. "You guys make the best coffee."

"That's because we're the only ones who still have coffee. What are the rest of you down to, now, instant?"

"Or chicory."

"Euw." Kim made a face. "Is there even caffeine in that?"

Harper looked around. Kim couldn't tell if it was with disapproval. "Where's Ingrid?" she said.

"She'll be along in a second."

"I don't have a lot of time."

Kim felt a little put out that Harper was being so pushy, but she tamped it down. "Busy?"

"What do you think?"

Boy, the end of the world sure brought out the bitch in some people, Kim thought. She tried to cut the tension and picked up a whiskey bottle. "Drink?"

Harper paused. She looked around, as if to check that they were alone, even though they were miles from the nearest home. "It's early. I'm on duty."

"Sure," Kim said. "So, is that a yes or a no?"

Harper thought it over, then held out her coffee cup. "Just a little," she said.

Kim poured some whiskey into her coffee, then a drop in her own. They drank in silence.

"I thought we finished all your whiskey at the wake for your Dad the other day," Harper said.

"We still have some in storage."

"That's what I need to talk to you about."

"Our whiskey?"

"Among other things."

Kim frowned. "Which other things?"

"The things you've got in storage."

Kim didn't like the sound of that. She took a sip of coffee and decided it needed more whiskey. She added a dash, and offered the bottle to Harper, who declined. "You mean Dad?" she said.

"Is he in the meat locker?" Harper asked.

"Yeah," Kim said sheepishly, surprised at how embarrassed she felt.

"Then we need to discuss that, too."

"Ok," Kim said and gulped coffee so she wouldn't have to say anything else just yet.

"I need a complete inventory, Kim. Of everything. Not just what's in the meat locker."

"Ok."

"And I need it to be complete. If you make me come here and do it myself and there's discrepancies, that's going to be a problem."

Kim felt angered by Harper's tone but all she said was, "it will be complete."

"Of everything," Harper insisted. "Medicine, foodstuffs, ammunition, tools, everything that could be useful."

"Including the whiskey?" Kim said, unable to keep the edge out of her voice.

If Harper noticed the edge, she ignored it. "Yeah, including the whiskey."

"Books?"

"Don't worry about the books."

"Why? Because most people in the valley can't read?" There was an even sharper edge in her voice that Kim hadn't intended, but found she couldn't prevent.

"Because we've still got a pretty good library, that's why, Little Miss Snoberooni," Harper said.

"Ok," Kim said, feeling a little chastised. "What else? Tampons?"

Harper let an edge creep into her own voice, now. "You think it'll go well for you if people learn you've been holding out on them?"

Kim didn't like the threat implied in that. "Everybody came here the other day and drank our whiskey and pretended to be sad about Dad's passing and now they want our stuff?" she complained.

"People wanted to pay their respects," Harper said, suddenly gentle.

"People wanted to drink our whiskey. It is *our* whiskey, you know. *Our* books. As is everything else. Including the tampons."

"It *was* yours," Harper insisted. "Nothing is yours anymore, Kim. Nothing belongs to any of us. You know that."

Kim drank her coffee, letting it sit in her mouth for a moment before swallowing, feeling the whiskey burn her palate pleasantly before feeling it warm her throat and stomach. "What kind of an insult is 'little Miss Snoberooni'?" she said.

"Where's Ingrid?" Harper said.

"She'll be along."

"I've got to get going. Tell her – "

Harper broke off as Ingrid stepped onto the gallery from the house, her hair wrapped in a towel, a coffee cup in her hand, her naked body dripping wet.

Chapter Seven

Donnie had been the first they'd lost, barely a mile from the city. Marauders in a pick-up truck bore down on them, and they'd all made a break for the woods. The brown leaves and dead trees didn't make for much cover, but at least the marauders couldn't follow in the truck.

As they ran, they crashed through the branches and underbrush, ran over a dry riverbed and a dry pond, and finally took cover amid the high weeds in what had once been a farmer's field. The marauders traipsed through the field after them, but there weren't enough of them to cover every inch.

It was almost dawn when they finally emerged from the weeds to regroup. It was only then that they realized Donnie was no longer among them. They found no trace of him, and Troy wondered just what exactly the marauders planned to do with him.

Already, before they'd left the city, there had been rumors of cannibalism.

Chapter Eight

Harper and Kim both looked at Ingrid for a moment, who casually sipped her coffee, water pooling on the deck at her feet, wearing nothing but the towel around her hair.

"Tell me what?" Ingrid said, casually, between sips.

Harper cleared her throat and said, "Hi, Ingrid."

Kim just said, sharply, "Ingrid."

Ingrid looked at her sister, pretending to be surprised by her tone. "What?"

"Could you put something on?" Kim said.

"You didn't tell me to put anything on," Ingrid said. "You told me to take a shower and drink some coffee." She turned to Harper. "You want coffee?"

"I've got some," Harper said.

"Ok." She turned to her sister, feigning mystification at the expression on Kim's face. "What?

"We have a guest and you're completely naked."

"I'm not completely naked," Ingrid said. She took the towel from her hair and flung it to the deck. Her dark, wet, and stringy hair bounced to her shoulder. "*Now* I'm completely naked."

Kim felt enraged. The passive-aggressiveness of her sister, when she knew how important this meeting was, drove her batshit.

Kim was also a little jealous of her sister and her perfect, still-under-twenty-five-year-old body, her perky boobs, her tight little tush, and her long legs, so immaculately smooth, while Kim was far too busy tending the fields and ensuring their survival to manage to shave her legs or armpits on a weekly, much less daily, basis.

"The Council is taking half of the field, guys," Harper blurted out.

This was met by a long silence.

"Oh," Kim said. "Ok." She paused and sipped her drink while she thought of what to say next. She felt bile roil in her stomach. "Which half?"

"We'll take the half on the other side of the creek," Harper said, "but we'll need to put in an access road so we can reach it from County Road Seven."

"Ok," Kim said, resigned.

"And we need to see you're making productive use of the rest of the field, Kim, or else we'll take that too."

Ingrid had heard enough. "It's our field," she protested.

"It's not," Harper said with authority. "Nothing is yours anymore, Ingrid. How do you think the rest of the valley feels, seeing you up here in your house with your electricity and your hot water and your whiskey?"

"We don't have hot water just now, actually," Ingrid said. "And how can they see us up here? Are they spying on us?"

"They were all here the other day for the wake," Harper said.

"They weren't *all* here," Ingrid said. "The entire valley wasn't here. What'd the people who were here do? Run back and tell the rest of them we've still got whiskey and toilet paper?"

"Everyone can see the lights blazing at night," Harper said. "You're the only private house in the valley with electricity. People can see your house for miles around. Everyone's scraping by, and you're living it up, up here."

"Dad put in solar panels," Ingrid said. "A water filtration system. Stocked up on antibiotics and antivirals. And toilet paper. And duct tape. A lot of duct tape. Dad made preparations. He made this place sustainable. No one else had the foresight to do that. And now we're being punished for it?"

"You're not being punished for it. We're still letting you

live here."

"*Letting* us?" Ingrid was outraged. "It's *our* house."

"The Council can take it away in a heartbeat."

"It's *our* house. You've been a guest in this house. You used to babysit us in this house. We all used to go skinny-dipping down in the creek together."

"You have to show you're doing your part. It's not just about you anymore, Ingrid."

"Why is everyone so obsessed with what we're doing here?" Ingrid complained. "Lowry has more shit than we do up on his compound on the mountain."

"Lowry ran out of propane six months ago," Harper said. "Your home and the clinic are the only places with electricity now."

There was a long silence while Ingrid glowered.

"We'll do our part," Kim said.

Ingrid was having none of it. "Your ass will do its part," she said.

"Ingrid," her sister said, sharply.

"It's our house," Ingrid said. "Our field."

"No," Harper insisted. "Not anymore."

"Who put the Council in charge?" Ingrid demanded.

"Well, the Council *is* in charge," Harper said.

"Of the county. Does the county have the power of eminent domain?"

"The Council is the authority, now. There's no one else."

"I think the thing of it is," Ingrid hesitated, trying to remember the speech she had practiced. "... the multitude of . . . factors. . . I mean, mitigating factors . . . multitudinous factors of utter mitigation-osity. Which is to say . . ."

Her mind drifted hopelessly into a black hole, and Ingrid stopped talking.

Harper stared at her for a few moments. "Are you high?" she asked, finally.

"Your ass is high," was all Ingrid could think to say.

"Ingrid's a little emotionally vulnerable since we lost

Dad," Kim explained. Ingrid resented her sister for forcing her to make excuses on her behalf.

Harper took a deep breath and let it out slowly before speaking. "I loved your father, Ingrid," she said. "I love you guys. You know that. I'm about the only one in the valley with genuine affection for you guys. But you're not the only ones to have lost someone. I mean, as far as we can tell, most of the world outside this valley is dead or dying or fighting to stay alive. Everyone has lost someone. You're not unique. You're not special. And you don't get special consideration. We've got a chance here. To make it. As a community. We've got things other communities didn't have, or weren't able to resource in time. If the Council doesn't see productive use of your property, you're going to have the entire field confiscated."

"Ok," Kim said, cautiously.

"Pot cultivating is not productive use of the property," Harper said.

Ingrid didn't like the sound of this. "Who says?"

"Ingrid," Kim said sharply.

"Cannabis has medicinal properties," Ingrid said.

Harper just glared at her, clearly not in the mood to discuss the medicinal properties of cannabis.

"We can do it better," Kim said, suddenly. "With the irrigation system Dad put in, we can make more productive use of the field than the County can."

"It's already been decided," Harper said. "Tomorrow we'll start planting in the far half of the field."

"The day after tomorrow," Ingrid blurted out. "Give us a day to harvest the marijuana crop."

Harper thought it over. "Ok," she said. "I can do that."

Chapter Nine

Within a week, Troy, Lilly, Gus and Roy had used all their water. It took them two days to find potable water, and even then, it was brackish and smelled of Sulphur.

By this time, they'd lost Tammy. As they'd neared an abandoned town, men in a black van emerged from a side street and gave chase. They ran into the woods and hid, but Tammy wasn't fast enough. For hours they lay hidden, listening to her cries.

When the marauders left, Troy, Lilly, Gus and Roy emerged from their hiding places, they found Tammy, her clothes ripped off, lying battered, in the fetal position. She didn't say what had happened to her – she refused to say anything at all – but it was easy enough to guess.

Tammy walked with them, mutely, for several days more, but then just sat down on the side of the road and never got up. They stayed with her as long as they could, but they couldn't carry her, so, eventually, they had to leave her behind.

Roy was next. He got sick. No one knew what he had, nor how to treat him, and everyone was afraid of getting sick themselves. They left him by the side of the road, in what little shade was provided by the bare branches of a tree.

There were three of them now, Troy, Lilly, and Gus. Gus was tall and muscular. He'd been in the military and was going to college on the GI bill. He was a little bit older. Troy felt a little bit safer with him around. A little bit.

They kept going, still moving at night when the air was

humid and stifling, resting during the day when the sun heated the blacktop to oven-like temperatures. Breathing in the air outside of the shade at those times was like breathing in the heat from a furnace. But it was hard to find shade through the bare branches of dead and dying trees.

They rationed their food, but, eventually, that ran out too. They stopped at abandoned gas stations and rest stops, but everything had been ransacked. They went without food and with barely any water. The woods disappeared into fields, mostly agricultural but long since gone fallow, overgrown with weeds that themselves were brown and dry and burned by the relentless sun. They passed some abandoned industrial farms, manure pits high and baked in the sun, chickens and pigs long since left to die in their pens, bodies by now mummified. They passed some family farms too, but those too were abandoned, and picked over by scavengers. At one, they found the bodies of a family, flesh rotted off their skeletons, still in their clothes, lying in their front yard and on their front steps where they had been cut down by what looked like a shotgun, judging by the pattern of the blast.

Despite the evidence of marauders and scavengers, they didn't see another living soul for weeks. Eventually, they came to a town that evidently had been largely wiped out by one of the diseases unleashed from the melting permafrost as it made its way south, or one of the tropical diseases that had worked its way north. The local clinic was filled with corpses, and, in most of the houses, the dead lay in their beds.

Miraculously, only the houses closest to the road had been ransacked; Roy supposed the multitude of corpses had kept scavengers at bay. The place must have stank at one point, but now the dead were beyond decay. Even so, the smell of their decomposition permeated the houses.

They scouted the houses all that day and chose one far back from the others and from the road. It was amply provisioned, but only contained one corpse. They dragged it to a storage shed; none of them had the strength to dig a hole in the baked hardpan earth.

Through a back yard of dead, brown grass, there shimmered an in-ground pool. It was filthy, the water green. They skimmed the surface as best they could, but the water remained unswimably fouled.

Inside the house, however, they found gallon jug upon gallon jug of clean, clear water, stacked on shelves in a basement storage room, along with rows upon rows of canned goods. After the disappointment of the pool, the temptation proved irresistible. They took several jugs out into the yard and the three of them stripped off their clothes and poured water over each other's naked bodies.

Afterwards, they soaked their greasy, sweat-caked clothes in water they poured into a washbasin, and laid them out to dry in the sun, while they sat in the shade of the back porch to let their bodies dry in the air. This proved difficult – the heat was such, even in the shade, that they never dried off, their perspiration welling up from their flesh as the water from the jug refused to evaporate in the humidity.

There was no electricity, but there was plenty of food in the pantry, so they ate cold chili directly from the can and drank bottled water and slept with a roof over their heads for the first time since they left the city. The house was hot and stifling, even with the windows open, but it was better than sleeping outdoors.

Troy and Lilly made love that night for the first time since they'd left their dorm. Afterwards, they discussed Gus. Lilly worried about him being all alone.

The next night, Lilly went to Gus in his bed. Troy didn't like it, but he wasn't as upset as he'd imagined. For all they knew, they could be the last three people on earth any of them would ever know, and no one, Troy thought, should have to be alone.

The next night, the three of them went to bed together. To Troy's surprise, there was very little awkwardness, and they soon found their rhythm. In the morning, there wasn't any regret. It had felt right.

Things were different after the apocalypse, Troy thought.

The next day, their strength revived, they waited until the sun went down and then dug a hole in the yard and buried the corpse of the man who had owned the house. Later, Troy played his backpacker guitar softly, and they sang songs – Johnny Cash and Woody Guthrie and Lennon and McCartney – quietly, so as not to attract marauders.

They worried about disease. None of them knew what had killed the people in this town, and none of them knew if the corpses were contagious.

Even so, it was tempting to think about staying in this house, about building a life, such as it was. They had shelter, they had food, they had water. When they ran out, they could scavenge in the other houses – unless scavenging among the corpses would expose them to the disease that had ended this town.

How long could they stay here? How long would they have to? Would this crisis pass? Or was this the world from here on out? What kind of life could they build surrounded by corpses? Could they live out their lives here? Was there enough food and water to last that long? Would they have a kid, eventually? Would they know who was the father? Would it matter?

How could they raise a kid in a house surrounded by the dead?

The next day, Gus began to cough.

Chapter Ten

After Harper left, Ingrid said, "she used to bring us presents. Do you remember when she used to babysit for us? She always brought a present. Why didn't she bring us a present?"

Kim turned to her sister and said, "What's wrong with you?"

"What's wrong with me?" Ingrid responded, outraged. "What's wrong with *you*?"

"What's wrong with *me*?" Kim replied, incredulous.

"I don't know," Ingrid said. "What *is* wrong with you, anyway? You're not protecting Daddy's legacy."

Ingrid saw her sister's eyes flash and her nose flare. "I – Jesus," she stammered. "How dare you!"

Ingrid swept her arms in an expansive gesture, taking in everything around them. "This is Daddy's legacy! This house! These fields! This way of life!"

"That is not Daddy's legacy!" Kim was yelling now. She began to wave her arms madly back and forth between herself and her sister. "We are Daddy's legacy! You and me! Will you please put on some clothes?"

"This is my house!" Ingrid insisted. "I'll do whatever I want in my own house and on my own property!"

"It's my house too!"

"You're not the boss of me!" Ingrid thundered. She glowered, farted, and stormed back into the house.

Kim stood on the gallery for a long time, trying to decide

how she was going to harvest the marijuana crop by herself.

Chapter Eleven

By nightfall, Gus was shivering with fever. He demanded Troy and Lilly go, before they caught what he had. Leave him as they had left the others, he insisted. They refused to do so. Things were different now.

Troy felt awful that they had left Tammy and Roy, but now wouldn't leave Gus. He supposed, thirsty and starving on the road, if they had stayed with Tammy or Roy, they'd all be dead by now. Perhaps they'd be dead if they stayed with Gus, too. He wondered if the reason they stayed with him was because, on some level, they didn't want to leave the shelter of this amply provisioned house.

In the end, it came to the same thing. Within two days, Gus was dead.

Lilly and Troy buried Gus in the yard beside the owner of the house, filled their backpacks with as much food and water as they could carry, and left, hoping they hadn't caught what had killed Gus and everyone else in the town.

For three weeks, they didn't see another soul. The plains gave way to the foothills, and ahead loomed a mountain range. What towns they saw were ruined – burned out, or deserted, or looted, or filled with the dead, corpses rotting away inside their homes. It looked like they were walking through a war zone. Which, Troy supposed, in a way, they were.

They were hopeful they'd avoided whatever infection had killed Gus. They figured if they were going to get sick, it would have happened by now.

The next day they walked uphill for hours until they faced a sign that informed them "the valley" was twenty miles further. Troy liked the idea of a valley. It sounded hopeful.

Then they heard a noise and turned to see a pick-up truck, still some distance away, bearing down on them.

Troy suggested they should run and hide.

Lilly told him she was too tired to run. Whatever was coming, she said, she was prepared to face it.

Troy looked at the truck and tried without success to make out the people riding in it.

Perhaps they were decent people, he thought.

Maybe they would help.

Chapter Twelve

Harper was on patrol when she got the call.

Although they had tanker trucks of gasoline under guard, Harper was acutely aware that once their fuel supplies were exhausted there was no way for them to be replenished. Even so, she kept the patrol cars gassed up and sent them out daily. It was worth it, she figured. People needed to see there were still people out there protecting them.

So, when the call came, she was travelling down Rural Route Ten, looking at the withered stalks of corn in the fields of the Gerald farm.

They were lucky there'd been relatively little major mining operations or corporate farming or industry in the valley over the years, she was thinking. What kept them poor then might help keep them alive now. They still had relatively clean water, aquifers, wells, lakes, streams, and creeks. But water tables were falling with the drought and some wells and creek beds are already dry. The upside of having no more winter was that they had a three hundred and sixty-five day growing season. The downside was, they didn't have a spring run-off anymore. Water-use was a big issue. They had good soil in the valley, but they had to be mindful of the crops they grew and the livestock they raised, to sustain arability and maximize the nutritional value of what they produced. There wasn't enough gasoline to run combines or tractors, so they had to do it the old-fashioned way. Mass irrigation was probably out of the question. They had to grow more drought resistant crops.

Harper wondered about coal. She had no idea if there were unexploited deposits in the mountains surrounding the valley, or if the reason there had been little mining here was because there wasn't that much coal to be found. Certainly, people had mined coal in the days before electricity, so there was no reason they couldn't do so again with the simple technology they still had. Could equipment in the valley be retrofitted to run on coal? And would it be worth the cost? They couldn't afford the environmental damage coal mining had caused in the past. If they fouled their water, they would all be dead soon enough, coal or not.

The radio squawked. It was Dawkins, at one of the two checkpoints leading in and out of the valley.

"Sheriff," he said. "You better get down here, pronto."

Chapter Thirteen

Four of her men aimed carbines at a naked young man who kneeled on the asphalt, his hands behind his head.

"How long has he been like that?" Harper asked.

"I don't know," Dawkins said. "Twenty minutes?"

"In the hot sun?" Harper said. "With his bare knees on the asphalt?"

Without waiting for an answer, Harper went to her Crown Vic, opened the trunk, and took out a pair of latex gloves and a surgical mask. She put them on and approached the man.

"Be careful, boss," Dawkins said.

"I don't think he's hiding any weapons, deputy," Harper said. Whether or not he was carrying a communicable disease, she thought, was another question.

Harper approached the young man. His shoulders were burned red.

"My name is Harper," she said, extending her hand.

The young man looked at her suspiciously a moment, then unfolded his hands stiffly from the back of his head and took her hand.

"I'm Troy," he croaked, dryly.

Harper helped him to his feet.

Harper took Troy to Doc Wilson's and put him in an examining room and, while Doc Wilson looked him over, Harper interrogated him, making him repeat his story over and over again, looking for inconsistencies.

After five hours, she pronounced herself satisfied.

In the interim, Doc Wilson ran what tests he could and returned to give Troy a clean bill of health, as far as his limited means could determine. But he cautioned that the young man should stay on antibiotics and antivirals for ten days as a precaution.

"I'll get a supply from the dispensary," Doc Wilson said.

"Don't bother," Harper said. "I know where we can get some."

Chapter Fourteen

It was close to evening when Harper showed up with the naked dude.

Ingrid herself was naked, too. She said it had something to do with being on strike or something. She vowed not to put on clothes again until the Council returned the confiscated half of their land. When she said it, Kim rolled her eyes.

The naked dude was dangerously skinny and stood with his hands awkwardly at his sides. He looked about Ingrid's age, early twenties, but Kim couldn't be sure if the partial emaciation made him look older or younger than his years. He stood with Harper on the lawn, while Kim and Ingrid observed them from the gallery.

"This is Troy," Harper said. "He's a refugee."

"From his pants?" Ingrid asked.

"From the city," Harper said. "He was robbed on the way into the valley."

"Ok," said Kim.

"*'Why, what could she have done, being what she is?'* Ingrid said, in a declamatory fashion. "*'Was there another Troy for her to burn?'*"

Harper and Kim looked at her like she was nuts.

"That was Yeats," Troy said.

"Bingo!" Ingrid said. "I like you, Troy."

"That's good, because Troy will be boarding with you," Harper said. She looked at Ingrid, critically. "Maybe you can start a nudist colony."

"We're taking in boarders?" Ingrid asked.

"Everyone in the valley has taken in boarders," Harper said. "Do you think you're special?"

"No," Kim interjected.

"Yes," Ingrid insisted.

"You're not special," Harper said. "Everybody has to do their part. This is a crisis. Haven't you noticed?"

"Your ass is a crisis," Ingrid said.

"Ingrid," Kim said, sharply.

"You're making *your* crisis *our* crisis," Ingrid told Harper. "We're fine. We're self-sufficient. If we never saw another living soul, Kim and I could sustain this place for a hundred years. We have electricity. Dad put in a system that recycles most of our water. And our well goes deep into the aquifer. We don't need your help and we don't want to give you any."

"We're all in this together," Harper said, teeth gritted. "You need to give Troy a ten-day supply of Cipro."

"Does he have anthrax?" Ingrid said.

"It's a precaution. You need to take antibiotics for ten days as well. Antivirals, too, for all three of you."

"Cipro makes me fart," Ingrid said, and farted.

"Everything makes you fart," Kim said.

"Troy, for ten days, don't leave this farm," Harper said.

"What about our pigs?" Ingrid said with alarm. "If he has anthrax, he'll kill our pigs."

"It's just a precaution," Harper said. "But for now, I'd keep Troy away from your pigs."

There followed a long pause as Harper and Ingrid glared at one another, and Troy stood there, awkwardly.

Kim approached the young man. "Troy, welcome to our home. Please come with me, I'll show you the shower and find you some clothes."

Chapter Fifteen

When Harper arrived back in town, she saw one of the Tilly boys strung up by his feet, hanging upside down outside the general store, while the proprietor, Gil Sullivan, beat him with a broom.

Harper slammed the brakes and scrambled out of the Crown Vic, her hand on the butt of her sidearm.

"Sully, you leave that kid alone or so help me I'll put a bullet in your fat ass," Harper said.

When Harper spoke, in general, people listened.

Sully looked at her, in high dudgeon. "Sheriff, I'm only hitting him with the bristles," he explained, showing her the broom. "It's better than he deserves. He stole from me."

It didn't really matter that he'd stolen. It wasn't Sully's place to take the law into his own hands. Still, Harper figured she'd better be even-handed in this matter.

"What'd he steal?" Harper asked, cautiously.

"Just a can a' beans," the kid said, through a nose made stuffy from hanging upside down.

"And a can of baby formula," Sully added. "You know what baby formula is worth these days?"

The baby formula raised all sorts of red flags for Harper.

"Sully," she said, firmly and evenly. "You let this kid down gently and you let him down now."

Harper sat with the kid in the Crown Vic. "You're Raymond Tilly, right?" she said.

"Everyone calls me Junior," the kid said. His father, Raymond Senior, had been one of the men who never returned from the raiding expedition Harper had organized at the beginning of the collapse. He'd left behind a pregnant wife and six kids. Junior, the oldest, was ten. They lived over in Melzingah Hollow, about an hour away. Harper could only imagine how long it had taken Junior to walk to the county seat.

"Junior," Harper said. "What's going on? Why're you stealing baby formula?"

"My mom's sick," Junior said. "She's not making enough milk for the baby."

"What's she got?"

"I don't know, Sheriff."

Ok, Harper thought. Time to get Doc Wilson on the case.

"You hungry?" she asked.

"No," the kid said.

"You eaten lately?"

"I ate yesterday," Junior said, bravely.

Harper took a deep breath. "You come with me," she said.

Chapter Sixteen

Troy couldn't believe he was taking an actual shower with actual hot water. He would have liked to have run the water really hot, but his burned shoulders wouldn't allow it. Even so, it was the best feeling ever to take a shower. He couldn't remember the last time he'd had one. When he finished, he was clean in a way he hadn't been since . . . *before*.

The one named Kim had left clothes folded neatly for him. He put them on. They were work clothes – strong fabric, but reasonably lightweight. He supposed they'd be putting him to work. He knew he'd better make an effort. He didn't want to give anyone a reason to send him back out on the road.

He could barely put on the shirt – his burned shoulders were too tender. But the underwear felt amazing. He'd forgotten how good clean underwear could feel.

He couldn't believe how lucky he was. He wished Lilly could have made it to the valley too. He tried not to think about it. He was too exhausted to allow himself to feel those emotions.

Dressed, Troy walked into the hallway. He saw a door ajar and approached it. As he neared, he heard the sound of a woman quietly sobbing. He turned from the sound and tiptoed back down the stairs.

He saw the one called Ingrid, still nude, sitting on a couch and strumming a guitar.

She stopped when she saw him.

"Those are Daddy's clothes," she said. "Are you wearing

his underwear, too?"

Troy said, "Kim left them for me."

"It's disrespectful," Ingrid said. "It's ghoulish."

"Is your father . . . ?"

"Dead?"

"Is he?"

"Yes," Ingrid said. She turned away and thoughtfully strummed her guitar. "I thought you were him for a second. You look a little like he used to look when he was younger. What can I get you? To drink. We have whiskey. We have beer."

"I'd kill for a beer," Troy said.

Ingrid looked up. "Whom will you kill?"

"What?"

"For the beer? Are you offering? Are you threatening?"

Troy was mortified. "It's an expression."

"Oh. You mean figuratively."

"I'm sorry. I didn't mean to scare you."

"You totally did not scare me."

"Ok," Troy said.

"I'll get you that beer. Daddy made his own beer."

"Your Daddy was --- what? A survivalist?"

Ingrid scoffed. "Hardly. Our parents went off the grid back in, I don't know, a million years ago."

"They saw this coming?"

"No," Ingrid said. "Ha. That's funny. No. No one saw this coming. I mean, until they did. But Mom and Dad just wanted to get back to the land and grow marijuana, that's all. They were hippies. We pretty much were raised running around naked all the time."

"I'm sorry about your Dad," Troy said.

"Because he died?"

"Yes."

"Yeah." She sighed, staring off into space. "I mean, it was sort of a blessing, you know, because he was sick for a long, long time, since even before everything went to shit. And, you know, if Daddy hadn't gotten sick when he did,

Kim and I wouldn't have been back here when, you know . . . All the shit went down. I was away in college. Kim was done with college, she was in the Peace Corps. But Dad got real sick, and we came back to care for him. We were caring for him when everything went to hell. I can't imagine what Kim would have done in some third world shithole when the world came to an end. Then again, maybe it wouldn't have been that different over there from the way it is here." She looked at Troy, her eyes moist. "I'll get you that beer." She stood up. "It's Ok if you look at my ass, by the way," she said. "Everyone does. My ass is hella cute."

She walked away from him, into the kitchen. Troy tried not to look, but he did.

Her ass *was* hella cute, he thought. He noticed a tasteful, barbed wire tattoo on her lower back, above it.

Chapter Seventeen

Harper went to the school gymnasium. The first thing she did was open up a package of beef jerky for Junior. The kid ate a few bites, then sealed up the package.

"I'll save the rest for my brothers and sisters," he said.

Harper felt a lump in her throat. "Junior," she said. "You eat as much as you want. I'll make sure there's enough for everyone."

They went around the gym together with a shopping cart, loading up on supplies, including baby formula.

By the time they were finished, deputy Dawkins had arrived with Doc Wilson. They loaded up Dawkins's Jeep Rambler, and Junior and Dawkins climbed in.

Harper hung back with Doc Wilson for a moment.

"You tell me what she's got," Harper said.

"Will do," the Doc said.

"How're we doing on antibiotics and antivirals?"

"I figure we've got enough for general practice and, maybe, two more outbreaks," the doctor said. "If there's no more outbreaks, we can treat the population for decades with what we've got."

Harper thought that over. "So, what's our plan?"

"Pray we don't have any more outbreaks," Doc Wilson said, and climbed into the Rambler.

Harper went to the Rambler to talk with Junior.

"You tell your Mom if she needs anything, get word to me," she said. "No one starves in the valley, Junior. No one."

Chapter Eighteen

It was good beer, Troy thought, as he sipped it slowly. Ingrid had said her father made his own beer. He wondered if his daughters knew how to make beer now that their father was gone. It had never occurred to him that beer could still be a thing in the world. Now that he had one in his hand, he wanted it to always be a thing.

Troy felt suddenly dizzy and sat down hard on the couch. He felt nauseous. He put his head between his legs.

He felt a hand on his shoulder.

"Ow," he said.

"Sorry." It was Kim. He looked up at her. Her eyes were red from crying.

"You shouldn't be drinking beer without eating something," she said, and handed him a plate of cold chicken.

It was the best thing he'd ever eaten, or at least felt that way.

"Don't rush," Kim said. "You'll make yourself sick."

Troy did his best to eat slowly.

When he finished, he felt restored, but also dead tired.

"You've got schmutz in your beard," Kim laughed, and wiped his mouth with a cloth napkin. When she finished, she regarded him. "You look like a hipster."

Troy raised an eyebrow. "Do we have those anymore?"

Kim frowned. "I'm not sure."

"I did have a t-shirt with Johnny Cash flipping the bird

at San Quentin."

"Oh, then you are totally a hipster."

"They took it when they . . . you know. They took everything."

They were quiet for a moment.

"I don't normally wear a beard, though," Troy said. "I mean, that was just because I couldn't shave."

Kim looked thoughtful. "You want to get rid of it?"

"I don't know," Troy said. "What do you think?"

"Well, you might find it useful for storing snacks and such. We have some venison jerky strips that would fit nicely."

Troy smiled. "So, you think I should get rid of it?"

"I think it will be very hot working out in the fields with us with that beard."

"OK," Troy said. "I'll shave."

"No," Kim said. "Let me do it."

Chapter Nineteen

Exhausted, Harper stopped off at the Silver Dollar Saloon and Grill.

The grilling was done out back on a wood-fired stove now, and the most affordable drink was now moonshine or applejack, but the place was still in business. Most exchange was done on the barter system these days. Harper refused to take payment from individuals for her law enforcement activities, although as compensation, the Council authorized her to provide herself with ample necessities from the supplies in the school gymnasium, and also set up a predetermined amount of credit at most of the vendors in the county seat.

The Silver Dollar, however, was not one of them. But since Harper's mother was one of the few beekeepers in the valley, and since the bee colonies, while depleted, had not been wiped out, Harper could buy pretty much anything she wanted and then some with a jar of honey. Harper made regular deliveries to the Silver Dollar, and she could eat and drink there to her heart's content.

Right now, all she wanted was some good Scotch. She didn't have a taste for moonshine, and while some of the local applejack was quite good, Scotch remained her preferred libation. The cost was prohibitive to most residents of the valley, but with no one processing sugar, honey was worth more than gold.

Harper ordered Laphroig and told Bart, the proprietor, to leave the bottle. She sat at the table and drank. She looked around the room. She recognized most of the people in it –

Ebert Rollings and his wife, Lacey; Scotty Hubbard, a few years her junior, who had once dated Kim; and Henry Lowry, looking imperious and imperial.

To her dismay, Henry Lowry approached her, a beveled glass in one hand and a bottle of Jack in the other. Harper liked the charcoal-filtered taste of JD, but it always gave her a headache, so she tried to stick to her single malts.

Lowry was the richest man in the valley, mostly because he owned a lot of land and had once charged a lot of rent to the people who either farmed it or lived in his several trailer parks. Before the collapse, Harper had spent more than enough time demanding that he reverse orders of eviction until after the required ninety-day wait and a properly issued Warrant of Eviction signed by a judge. Unfortunately, she often wound up overseeing the same eviction once the ninety days and the required seventy-two-hour notice had passed.

Lowry lived in a compound on the mountain, not far from the reservoir. He had over a dozen men up there with him. In another era, they'd have been referred to as "gun thugs." Like Ingrid and Kim, Lowry had stockpiled a lot of supplies up there. Unlike the sisters, he'd never installed solar panels, so once his propane had run out and he could no longer run his backup generators, he lived without electricity, like most of the valley. He'd been demanding the Council provide him with propane, but Harper insisted propane to run generators had to be reserved for the clinic, fire department, and the Sheriff's offices.

The Silver Dollar had been in business since the 19th century, and the proprietors had always made an effort to maintain something approximating the original décor – wood paneled walls, mahogany bar, leather and wood barstools. Now, since most of the usable technology was 19th century, entering the saloon really did feel like stepping back in time, with lanterns lighting the dark interior. Lowry, himself dressed in a vest and a flat-top derby, only reinforced that impression.

"Evening, Sheriff," Lowry said, sitting down at her table. "Mind if I join you?"

Harper lifted her glass and regarded Lowry over the lip,

the amber liquid glimmering in the dim kerosene light.

"If I said I did, would it make any difference?" Harper asked.

Lowry laughed, even though Harper suspected he knew she wasn't joking.

Lowry pulled up a chair and sat across the table from her. "I heard you allowed in a refugee today," he said.

"Gossip is the Devil's radio," Harper said.

Lowry screwed up his face, trying to place the quote.

Harper gave him an assist. "George Harrison."

"Ah," Lowry said, thoughtfully. "More of a Toby Keith man, myself."

Of course you are, Harper thought, and sipped her Scotch, feeling its comforting burn in her throat and belly. "A young man arrived at the checkpoint today, yes," Harper admitted. "He's been vetted, examined, and boarded."

"You're pretty confident he's not going to infect us all with something?"

"Doc Wilson gave him a thorough looking over, and he's on a ten-day regimen of Cipro."

"What I'm wondering about, Sheriff, is allocation of resources."

Harper let that hang in the air a moment.

"Yes?" she said, finally.

Lowry refilled his glass. "You sent a trunk full of supplies to the Tilly family in Melzingah Hollow, is that right?"

"That's right."

"Are you planning to send any foraging expeditions outside the valley anytime?" Lowry said. "Looking for Walmarts that haven't been looted, that kind of thing?"

Harper narrowed her eyes. "What's your point, Henry?"

"Those supplies you've got under lock and key in the school gymnasium are a finite resource," Lowry said.

"No one starves in the valley, Henry," Harper said.

"From each according to his ability, to each according to his need, is that it, Harper?"

"You actually read Marx, Henry?" Harper said,

skeptically. "Or just the comic book version?"

"My concern, Harper, is that you're teaching people that they don't have to work for what they get," Lowry said, and sipped his JD. "That they're entitled."

Harper smiled, but it wasn't a happy smile. "It's funny how little some people's attitudes change," she said, "even after the world ends."

"People aren't entitled to free stuff, Harper."

"You want to abandon widows and orphans?"

"Junior is old enough to be put to work."

"He's ten. He should be in school."

"Not every kid needs to go to school, Harper."

"His father probably died helping to get the supplies that have continued to help sustain this valley since the collapse. His family deserves some gratitude, and a life-time of free food, as far as I'm concerned."

"It's very sad about Raymond Senior," Lowry said, "but since he never returned, he didn't actually contribute anything to the valley, did he?"

Harper sipped her drink, swallowed. She could feel the drink going to her head, making her feel a little surly. "I think we're done here."

"I need to make one thing clear to you, Harper."

"I'm really not interested."

"We need to restore the Constitution. We need to restore private property rights."

"There we have it," Harper said. "That's what this is about."

"The Council does not have the right to control my property or my resources."

"This from a man who thinks he's entitled to the County's propane?"

"I'm entitled to my fair share, yes."

"Which, undoubtedly, you think is much greater than anyone else's fair share. You think your vote should count double, as well?"

"I'm an important man in this part of the world, Sheriff," Lowry said.

"You're mistaken," Harper said. "You're not important. And you don't control any resources. The Council does. At best, you've been allowed to continue to manage some of them for us."

Lowry glowered, his face flushing with rage. "That's communism," he muttered.

"You need to do your part," Harper said. "Same as everyone else."

"What I need to make clear to you," Lowry said, "is that you don't want to test that proposition with me."

Harper stared at him hard. "Are you making threats now?"

"No threats. Just facts."

"You're going to do your part, Henry," Harper said. "Whether you want to or not."

Lowry smiled, sipped his drink, and stood up. "It's been nice catching up with you, Sheriff," he said.

Harper refreshed her drink and looked up at Lowry. "I'll need a full inventory of everything you've got up at your compound, Lowry. Every supply and every resource."

Lowry glowered. "That's not going to happen."

"I think it is," Harper said, and raised her glass.

"You're wrong, then," Lowry said.

"One of us is wrong," Harper said. "You need to think long and hard about which one of us that really is."

Chapter Twenty

Kim led Troy outside, and instructed him to take off his shirt. She sat him down at the picnic table, wrapped a bedsheet around his shoulders, and took a pair of scissors to his beard, trimming it down. This took a while. Then she moved on to his hair.

Then she disappeared into the house and reemerged with a basin of hot water, a brush and a pedestal of shaving cream, a strop and a straight razor.

"Wow," Troy said.

"Dad was old school," Kim said.

She lathered up his face, then sharpened the blade on the strop.

"You haven't seen *Sweeney Todd*, have you?" Todd asked.

"The play or the movie?" Kim said.

"Either one."

Kim smiled. "Both, actually."

Todd's face, which had brightened, took on a gloomy cast. "I guess that's not really funny. Because maybe people *are* actually cannibals now."

Kim stopped sharpening the razor. "Well," she said. "Not in this valley, anyway. Not yet."

She put the blade to his throat and began to shave him clean.

After a few moments of silence, she said, "What was it like?"

Troy, the blade scraping the stubble from his throat, said, "what do you mean?" even though he knew exactly what she meant.

"You know what I mean," Kim said. "I mean, everything. We're a little isolated here. We heard rumors, saw some stuff on TV, until the TV went dead. Some reports on shortwave . . . until that went dead too."

Troy took a deep breath.

"There were, like, half a dozen of us when we started out." He swallowed, his Adam's apple swelling against the blade. "I'm the only one left."

"The road was pretty bad?"

"It was, like, everyone who was left alive was an animal. Everywhere, people just wanted to rob and kill and rape you, pretty much. We got robbed. Beaten. And raped. And killed. They're all gone. All the rest of my group. No one helped us. Not a one. Until I got here. To the valley. And you guys." He paused, his throat choking with emotion. "Thanks for taking me in."

"It wasn't our idea," Kim said.

"Thanks anyway," Troy said.

Kim finished shaving. She took a towel, wet it, and put it to Troy's face, wiping away any residual shaving cream. "You look younger," she said. "And skinnier. We need to fatten you up." She removed the sheet and looked at his naked upper torso. "Hang on a sec," she said, and disappeared inside.

After a few moments, she returned with a jar.

"Hold still," she said.

She opened the jar. It smelled of aloe. She dipped her fingers into the jar and spread the gel on her palms. She put her hands to Troy's shoulders.

The gel stung for a moment, then a soothing sensation spread over his skin. The touch of Kim's hands on his bare flesh was unbearably tender and welcome.

When she finished, they waited in the gloaming for the gel to dry, then Kim helped him into his shirt. She stood back and regarded him.

"Dad's clothes fit you pretty well," she said.

Chapter Twenty-One

Harper lived in a small house on the edge of town.

When she arrived home, she went to the kitchen, turned on the taps in the sink, and filled a pot with water.

The pumping station up on the mountain was a 9th century relic, and while the newer equipment was no longer running, the manual valves could still be turned to allow gravity to bring clear, clean water from the reservoir to the town's homes. Harper also had an old-fashioned well in her yard, but she considered that back-up.

Most of the residents of the towns in the valley had running water, and those further out in the rural areas almost all had wells. That was the good news. How much longer the water would last – that was another question. The reservoir was in decent shape, but it had been higher in the past – much higher. The Council had imposed water use restrictions. Harper wondered if one day soon it would become necessary to shut down the flow of water for a certain number of hours every day. She wasn't entirely sure she knew how to accomplish that.

Harper put the pot on the stove and heated it up. Then she put on oven mitts and brought it upstairs. She stopped up the bathroom sink and slowly filled it with the water from the pot. While she waited for the water to cool a bit, she stripped naked. Once the water felt right, she began to give herself a sponge bath.

She'd managed to find a cast-iron tub which she'd put in the kitchen, so she didn't have to lug pot after pot of water upstairs to the bathtub. She was too tired and impatient to heat up that much water right now, however, and a cold shower didn't offer the comfort she desired.

As she ran the sponge across her shoulder, she felt a man slide in behind her, pressing his naked body to hers, wrapping his arms around her.

Chapter Twenty-Two

Back inside, Ingrid was still strumming her guitar, and still naked. When Kim and Troy came in, she looked up and examined her sister for a moment.

"You've been crying," Ingrid said, accusingly, with something that sounded like satisfaction, Troy thought.

"Shut up," Kim replied. "Put some clothes on."

"You've totally been crying," Ingrid insisted.

"Put some clothes on."

"No."

"We have a guest."

"This is my house. I'll wear what I want. Besides, our guest doesn't mind." She turned to Troy. "Do you?"

Troy didn't know what to say, so he didn't say anything.

Bored, Ingrid turned back to her sister. "Why were you crying?"

Kim took a breath. "Turns out, I'm more sentimental about which of Daddy's clothes to give away than I expected to be."

"Cry baby," Ingrid said.

"Fuck you," Kim said, and went upstairs.

Ingrid turned to Troy. "What was your major?"

"My major?" Troy repeated, taken aback.

"In college. You were in college, right? When everything went to shit? You were away at school?"

"Musicology," Troy said, embarrassed.

"Oh!" Ingrid squealed, delightedly. "So, you're what a musicologist looks like. Do you know this one?"

Ingrid began to play guitar and sing:

You ought to see my Cindy
She lives way down South
She's so sweet the honey bees,
Swarm around her mouth

Git along home Cindy, Cindy
Git along home Cindy, Cindy
Git along home Cindy, Cindy
I'll marry you some day

"John Lomax says that song originated in North Carolina," Troy said, as Ingrid continued to strum the guitar. "Originally probably sung by slaves in a version called 'Cindy Ann.' Nick Cave and Johnny Cash did this song on the *Unearthed* compilation."

"Yes, they did!" Ingrid exclaimed. She added, accusingly, "*hipster.*"

"That's what your sister called me. Because I used to have that t-shirt of Cash flipping the bird to the camera at San Quentin."

"Oh, you are definitely a hipster, then. A hipster musicologist."

"I guess musicology isn't the most useful profession to go into right now."

"Or hipster, I guess. Not that it ever was."

"You're a really good singer," Troy said.

"Thanks. Do you sing?"

"A little. I study music, I don't really perform it. Just for friends."

"Sing with me," Ingrid said.

"I don't know the words."

"Seriously?"

"I study music, but I don't always memorize it."

"Lame," Ingrid admonished.

"I had a professor in a lecture course, he actually did his dissertation on this song. Weird thing was, the guys in the pick-up truck that . . . um, stopped us? One of them looked a lot like that professor. Except with a big-ass beard. My professor didn't have a big-ass beard. His name was Foxx."

"Like the *Fox and the Hound*?"

"Double X."

"You mean the pornographic version of the *Fox and the Hound*?"

"No, I mean, he spells his name with two Xs."

Ingrid, who had been going through the chord changes as they spoke, could no longer contain herself. "Join me on the chorus when it comes around again, Ok?"

Ingrid sang the next verse. When the chorus came around, Troy joined her.

"You sing great!" Ingrid said when the chorus ended, continuing to play the chord sequence as she spoke. "Maybe we can find you a guitar and we can put on a show for the locals. Then maybe they won't lynch us for our antibiotics and our whiskey. You play guitar?"

"A little. I had one of those backpacker lightweights, you know? I took it with me when we left the city."

Ingrid frowned. "You expected to have time for a lot of entertainment during the collapse of civilization?"

"Well, I figured without electricity, whatever entertainment we had, we'd have to make it ourselves. Those guys took it, though."

"The guys in the pick-up truck?"

"Yeah."

"What else did they take from you?"

Troy paused.

"Everything," he said, in a hoarse whisper.

Ingrid strummed her guitar. "Did they rape you?"

Troy took a deep breath. "Ricky Nelson and Dean Martin also sing that song in *Rio Bravo*," he said.

"Oh! I think we have that on DVD!" Ingrid exclaimed. "We can still watch DVDs, because of our solar panels. We're, like, the only people in the valley with solar panels. Bring it on home with me, ok?"

She sang the next verse, and Troy finished up the chorus with her, which they repeated.

The song ended and the final chord rang out for what seemed like a long time. Night was falling and the shadows were long, but the heat had barely diminished.

"That backpacker guitar of mine," Troy said. "It had Pete Seeger's quote written on it: 'This Machine Surrounds Hate and Forces it to Surrender.'"

Ingrid thought that over for a few moments.

"Wouldn't it be lovely if that were true?" she said.

Chapter Twenty-Three

Harper didn't like to be snuck up upon. It was only when she recognized the feel of Daryl's chest against her back and his loins hardening against her buttocks, that she relaxed.

She'd given Daryl a copy of her house key, but she had begun to dislike the way he showed up without an invitation and waited for her to come home. She was considering taking the key back.

Still, she liked Daryl well enough. A former gas station attendant, when there still had been gas to pump, Daryl had been her on-and-off lover for years. He no longer smelled like gasoline as he used to, but every time he touched her, Harper could remember the smell. She found herself regretting its absence. She had begun to associate it with pleasure and a welcome distraction from the stress of her life.

She didn't love Daryl, and she didn't think he loved her. But they both filled a need in the other, and that was working out reasonably well. Harper had lovers both male and female over the years, and, before things had collapsed, she had started to think she may have a slight orientation towards lovers of her own gender. But in this rural community, it was hard to meet women who were willing to admit they shared her orientation. And so, Daryl continued to share her bed several nights a week. She had never shared Daryl's – she realized she had never even been to his house. She further realized she didn't really ever want to.

"Daryl," she said, as his muscular arms groped her torso.

"I'm all stinky."

Daryl put his face to her shoulder and inhaled deeply. "You smell fine," he assured her, and began to nibble on her neck.

To his credit, Daryl was not the kind of guy who expected women to be delicately perfumed and powdered damsels, which was good, because Harper was certainly neither one. She knew she was not his only lover. That made her feel free to take an additional lover or two of her own, which was something she thought she might do as soon as time permitted, but hadn't gotten around to yet.

Daryl caressed her breasts with one hand and, with the other, caressed her between her thighs with his calloused fingers. Soon, Harper forgot her reservations, as she turned and kissed Daryl hungrily.

Daryl dropped to his knees, grabbed her ass, and put his mouth between her thighs. When they had first started seeing each other, Daryl had to be coaxed to go down on her, and was pretty clumsy once he did. He no longer had to be coaxed. And he had developed a certain modicum of finesse.

Harper grabbed his hair and gasped as she felt herself grow warm and ready.

Daryl rose, and they kissed, hard. Harper could taste herself on his tongue. She braced herself against the sink and stood with her legs apart, thrusting her loins out to meet his. Gently, Daryl entered her from behind.

Harper usually preferred not to look into Daryl's face when they made love. He had a perfectly lovely face – handsome, rugged, a little bit of bad-boy roguishness, with his five o'clock shadow and the way his locks of curly hair fell onto his forehead. But she felt uncomfortable with the intimacy of looking at him as their bodies joined.

This time, however, she found herself looking at Daryl's face in the mirror as he thrust into her and she pressed back to meet him. Daryl had a look of intense concentration as they made love. He was staring hard at her tush. Harper found it charming and a little bit silly. It made her self-conscious, the attention Daryl always paid to her rump, which she thought was overlarge and not particularly attractive. But he had nothing but praise for her backside.

Daryl put one hand gently on her lower back tattoo, a barbed wire design she'd gotten at the age of sixteen. Ingrid and Kim, a few years younger than her, had *oo-ed* and *ah-ed* the first time they'd seen it during one of their skinny-dips in the creek on their father's property. Ingrid had gotten herself an identical one as soon as she turned sixteen, a few years later. Harper thought Ingrid's looked much better above her perfect little rear-end than Harper's did above hers.

Harper realized she was making love to Daryl and thinking about Ingrid. Ingrid, it seemed, occupied her thoughts much more than she should these days.

When Daryl closed his eyes and his head rolled back, she knew he was almost there. She put her hand to her sex and touched where their bodies met. As she felt her ardor rise, she felt the room warm almost unbearably as the heat of their bodies rose. Sweat pooled at her temples and ran into her eyes. It stung and she closed one eye. With the other, she continued to watch Daryl with almost scientific dispassion as he climaxed.

Daryl held her tightly to him as he emptied himself into her. Harper was grateful for the supply of birth control pills she still had access to, and wondered what they would do when it ran out.

Before Daryl finished, Harper felt herself climax. As she came, her thoughts drifted to images of Ingrid's lower back tattoo.

As her passion subsided, she turned to kiss him, biting his lower lip playfully.

She wondered when a good time would be to ask him for that key back.

Chapter Twenty-Four

At some point in the middle of the night, Troy was awakened by music blasting from downstairs.

He sat up with a start, half-dreaming, thinking he was on the road again and a pick-up truck filled with filthy, gun-toting men was bearing down on him, speakers in the cab playing "Cindy, Cindy."

He blinked and gradually the room that was spinning in his disorientation righted itself and he felt the soft mattress under him, and he remembered where he was.

He stumbled out of bed, lurched out the door, and down the stairs. His heart was slamming in his chest and his throat was dry. He wore only his underpants – not his underpants actually, a dead man's underpants – and he felt awkward about that, but he had terrible visions of intruders invading the house, and while he didn't know what he was going to do when he confronted them, he felt he had to do something, quickly.

When he arrived in the living room he was met by a massive blast of cold air and he saw Ingrid, still naked, dancing to Elvis's version of "Cindy, Cindy," a massive doobie in her hand, from which she occasionally toked.

Troy didn't know whether to be shocked or entranced. He supposed he was a little bit of both.

She was beautiful, he thought, but he didn't find the sight of her writhing about arousing so much as incomprehensible. She seemed utterly oblivious to his presence.

Suddenly, Kim was at his side, wearing a t-shirt and boxers.

"OhMyGod," Kim said, and marched into the room. She snapped off the stereo, then went to the thermostat and cut the air conditioning.

Ingrid turned to her, dumbfounded, blinking.

"Toke?" Ingrid said, offering the doobie.

Kim slapped her hand away and the doobie went flying into a corner.

"Hey!" Ingrid cried. She went to the corner and got down on her hands and knees, trying to retrieve the doobie from between the legs of a credenza. Her rump was thrust out in Troy's line of sight. He tried to look away, but couldn't quite bring himself to do so.

"What the hell are you doing?" Kim scolded her sister. "I told you we can't run the air conditioning!"

"It's hot!" Ingrid cried.

"We can't risk overloading the solar cells!"

"You just feel guilty we're the only ones with air conditioning!"

"People are trying to sleep!"

"I wasn't sleepy!"

"What do you think the rest of the valley is going to think when they see our house lit up like the Fourth of July with music blasting out of the windows?"

"I don't give a fuck what the rest of the valley thinks!"

Kim put her face in her hands. Troy wasn't sure if she was crying or trying to restrain herself.

Ingrid stood up, toking on the doobie. "Hey, I had a dream. Do you want to hear my dream?"

"No," Kim said.

"Why don't you want to hear my dream?"

"Will you just go to bed?"

"I dreamed that Harper brought us a naked dude to take care of and that you shaved his beard and I played guitar for him."

Kim looked up at her sister, teeth gritted, eyes narrowed.

Ingrid glanced over and saw Troy.

"Oh, shit," she said, realizing her dream wasn't a dream after all.

She held out the doobie to Troy.

"Toke?" she offered.

Chapter Twenty-Five

Harper was on patrol early the next morning when she got the call from Dawkins that there was a problem at the Dolan farm.

Hardscrabble farmers for generations, the Dolans had managed to sustain operations, on a somewhat curtailed basis, even after the collapse, and the crops, dairy, and meat they produced had become important to the valley's well-being. So, a problem at the Dolan farm was a problem for everyone.

When Harper arrived, she quickly saw the nature of the problem.

"I went out this morning and the creek was dry," Mrs. Dolan, the family's sixty-year old matriarch said.

Harper looked up the mountain from where the creek ran downhill.

Harper and Dawkins were breaking up the dam they found up-stream when Lowry arrived with three armed men.

"That's my creek, gentlemen," Lowry said.

Harper marched towards Lowry with purpose. Lowry smirked. Harper wanted to slap the smirk off his face. She opted for a right hook instead.

Harper had maintained a combat-ready physical condition ever since she left the armed service. She was tall for a woman, but beyond that, she was as strong as a good many men in the valley. Lowry's head snapped back, his eyes lost focus, and he flew off his feet and landed on his back.

His men reached for their sidearms.

Harper drew hers first.

"First one of you to clear leather is a dead man," Harper said, enjoying how much she sounded like a badass cowgirl.

The men hesitated. Dawkins had his own sidearm out, holding it two-handed, his finger on the trigger guard.

Lowry sat up, shook his head, put his hand to his mouth. She hadn't knocked out any teeth, but his lip was bleeding.

"Jesus Christ, Sheriff," he said. He sounded surprisingly mild.

"I don't think I fully impressed upon you the gravity of the situation when last we spoke Henry," Harper said, gently. "The water that runs through this valley is community property, even if it runs through yours. Any attempt to interfere with its flow will be considered a crime against the community and dealt with accordingly."

"You have no right," Lowry muttered.

"I have every right," Harper said. "But I'm not going to debate this with you. Next time I'll lock you up and bring charges. If you don't come willingly, I'll put a bullet in your ass, and that of any of your men who try to interfere. Are we clear?"

"Sheriff," Lowry said. "If it's a war you want, that's something I can provide."

"I'd advise against it," Harper said. "I guarantee you, it's a war you'll lose."

Chapter Twenty-Six

When Kim and Troy came in from the fields about noon that day, they found Ingrid as they'd left her when they went out at dawn – naked and passed out face down on the couch.

Kim stared at her sister in disgust for a few moments. Troy tried to look away.

"I'm going to wash up and get some lunch ready," Kim said, and disappeared into the kitchen.

Troy did not know what to do. He found his eyes drawn to the slope of Ingrid's back, the curve of her buttocks, the flesh of her thighs.

He took a deep breath and stepped out onto the gallery. Despite the shade, the heat of midday hit him. He sat down and looked out at the fields and the trees beyond.

He was amazed at how much green there was in the valley. Not that it was all green – a lot of it was withered and brown. But there was still a lot of green. Outside the valley, there was no green. Every tree, stalk, and blade of grass had all been drought-and-sun-blasted.

Suddenly, Ingrid was beside him, still nude.

"So, Baxter," she said.

Troy was confused. "Baxter?"

"Isn't that your name?"

"Troy."

"Troy is your name?"

"Since I was born."

"Are you sure?"

"Pretty sure."

"Huh." She sat down beside him on the porch swing. She lifted her leg and looked at her toenails. "I thought you were Dad for a second. I took you for him. You look like he used to. When I was a kid and he was coming in from tending the marijuana plants. You're wearing his things."

"Thanks for lending them to me," he said. She was making him so uncomfortable. He still didn't know if she was trying to be provocative, or if going naked was just her thing. She didn't seem interested in him. Maybe things were different now that the world had ended. Maybe the old conventions, like wearing clothes, were ridiculous.

"I didn't lend them to you," Ingrid said. "Kim did."

"Ok."

"Want to get stoned, Baxter?"

"Troy."

"Want to get stoned, whatever your name is?"

"Troy. It's Troy. My name is Troy."

"So, that's a, what, qualified 'yes?'"

"I think I should wait until the work for the day is done," Troy said. "I don't think Kim would like it if I got stoned now."

"Oh, Kim," Ingrid grumbled, lighting a huge doobie. "That bitch."

"I think she's nice."

Ingrid looked at him like he was insane. "You do?"

"Don't you?"

"She's my sister. I *know* she's not nice. She's bossy. You're Ok with bossy? Because if you are, then Kim is totally your gal."

"Well," Troy said. "Someone needs to be the boss, I guess."

Ingrid laughed, expelling smoke, and coughing a little. "What are you, a Republican?"

"Do we even have those anymore?" Troy wondered.

"You know, that's an excellent question," Ingrid said,

thoughtfully. "Harper tells me the Council has taken over, but, I mean, did they suspend elections? If not, when it comes time to run again, do they still have political parties? Or do they make up new ones?"

They were silent for a few moments, staring at the valley, contemplating the nature of politics post-apocalypse, as Ingrid toked.

"Do you have internet?" Troy asked.

"Internet," Ingrid repeated, dreamily.

"You know, since you're like the only people on the planet, practically, to still have electricity. I figured you maybe have a mobile broadband device or something?"

"The cell towers are all down," Ingrid explained patiently, staring into the valley. "Even before then, most of the servers were down. The few sites that were still up, they were ghosts. No one updating them. You're the most news we've had in weeks."

Troy thought that over.

"So," he said.

"Yes," Ingrid concurred. "This is life, now. I mean, you may or may not end up staying with us forever, but chances are, you will live out the rest of your life in this valley doing manual labor of some kind, probably growing crops or slinging pig slop."

Kim came out on to the gallery and glared at her sister.

"Troy," she said through gritted teeth, "why don't you wash up, and then we'll eat."

Quietly, Troy went inside.

Chapter Twenty-Seven

Ingrid watched Troy disappear into the house. "He's cute," she said.

"What the hell is wrong with you?" Kim exploded. She felt her heart pounding and her pulse racing.

Ingrid looked at her confused. "What?"

"Put some clothes on!"

"I'm on strike," Ingrid explained. "I'm not putting on clothes until you put on the air-conditioning."

"That is not why you're prancing around naked in front of Troy!"

"You think I like him?"

"No," Kim said, feeling her rage rise inside her. "I think you think *I* like him so you're going to get him to like you so he doesn't like me."

Having said it, it sounded petty and paranoid. Even so, Kim still knew it was true.

Ingrid took a big toke, held it in, let it out, and said, "so you *do* like him?"

"I didn't say that."

"He went to college and you can have a conversation with him. You could do a lot worse. It's not crazy to think about those things. If we want to get married and stuff, we're going to have to settle for someone in the valley."

Kim was taken aback. "You think I should marry him?" She'd just met the guy for fuck's sake.

"Why not?" Ingrid asked, innocently.

"He's not my type," Kim lied.

"Kim," Ingrid said, seriously. "Your type are all dead."

Kim didn't quite know how to respond to that. She had to admit Ingrid had a point, even if she wasn't going to admit it aloud.

Ingrid stood up, turned her back on her sister, lifted one leg, and farted, long and loud.

She turned around with a smirk on her face.

"I told you Cipro makes me fart," she said, smugly.

Kim wanted to throttle her, but didn't want to give her sister the satisfaction.

Chapter Twenty-Eight

Harper pulled the Crown Vic up the driveway to the front of the farmhouse and went around to the back. She could see Kim and Troy working in the field, but Ingrid was nowhere to be found.

She went indoors and called Ingrid's name. No answer.

She went outdoors again, and looked at Kim and Troy, slaving under the hot sun. She felt the perspiration soaking through the shirt on her back. It dripped down her forehead and stung her eyes.

Harper wondered if the solar panels really provided enough energy to run the meat locker. She decided to find out.

She went around the side of the house and into the basement. She walked by the rows and rows of canned and dry goods, and opened the door to the meat locker.

A wave of blissfully frozen air hit her face. She stepped inside.

"Hi," Ingrid said.

Harper took off her dark glasses, which had frosted over.

Ingrid was sitting naked on a metal folding chair across from the shrouded figure of her father, who lay on a shelf beside tubs of ice cream and slabs of slaughtered hog wrapped in butcher paper.

"What the hell is going on here?" Harper said.

"I come in here to cool off, sometimes," Ingrid said. "Kim won't let us run the air conditioning in the house. She says she doesn't want to stress the solar cells, but I think it's because she feels guilty being the only one in the valley with working air conditioning."

"Ingrid," Harper stammered. She didn't know where to begin. "You're sitting naked in a room with your dead father."

Ingrid pouted. "Don't make it sound all gross."

Harper pressed her case. "This can't be healthy. Hygienically or emotionally. You have pig and goat meat in here!"

"Also, venison, and frozen chicken and turkey. And ice cream! But I don't sit on the meat or in the ice cream, for God's sake."

"I'm not sure it's hygienic to store meat with a dead person and a naked girl."

"Don't be ridiculous," Ingrid said. "First of all, I'm not being stored here, I'm just visiting. Second, when our cat died, we kept her in the freezer until Kim came home from Spring break so we could all bury her together. So, it's perfectly fine."

Harper was not so sure. "I'm going to have to look into that."

"Are you going to ask the Council to order us to take Daddy out of the meat locker?"

Harper sighed. "I'm not going to do that."

"Just because we do things differently around here doesn't mean we don't do them with our own kind of integrity," Ingrid said. She sounded genuinely emotional, rather than merely petulant, Harper thought. "I don't want the Council judging us."

"No one's interested in judging anyone."

"Everyone around here's been judging us since we settled here and we all ran around naked all summer long, until Mom died. You remember. You were there. You did it with us. You were the only one who didn't judge us." Ingrid thought for a moment. "I wonder why we stopped doing that after Mom died."

"I think when your mom died, you all lost some of your joy," Harper said, sadly.

"Yeah," said Ingrid. "I guess we did." She was thoughtful

for a few moments, staring at her father's shrouded corpse. Then she turned back to Harper. "There's another chair over there," Ingrid said, pointing to the wall, where another metal chair stood folded. "Why don't you join me?"

"Oh, come on, Ingrid."

"What? We used to go skinny-dipping all the time with Kim."

"We were kids."

"The last time I was eighteen and you were twenty-six," Ingrid said. "And that was only a few years ago."

Harper gritted her teeth, but she had to admit the idea was tempting. She hadn't felt cool air like this since the grid went down.

"Turn away," she said.

"Why?" Ingrid said.

"Just turn around."

Ingrid made a big show of sighing and rolling her eyes, but she turned away.

Harper undressed quickly, putting her uniform, gun-belt, and underwear in a pile, then unfolded the metal chair and sat down upon it.

"Oh!" she exclaimed.

Ingrid turned back to her and laughed. "The cold metal is refreshing on your tushie, right?" she said. She looked at Harper with interest. "You still have really nice boobs, by the way."

Harper, embarrassed yet oddly pleased, tried to ignore the remark. "We need to talk about your Dad," she said, gesturing to the shrouded figure on the shelf.

"What about Daddy?"

"You can't feed him to the pigs."

"It was his dying wish," Ingrid said, seriously.

"His dying wish was to be transformed into pigshit?" Harper said. She felt ridiculous having this conversation under these conditions, but there she was.

"Circle of life and all that."

"It's out of the question. You don't have to bury him in town, but you have to bury him. Or burn him."

"He wanted us to feed him to the pigs."

"People don't want to eat pigs that have eaten people. It's kind of a pretty obvious thing."

"We haven't offered our pigs for anyone to eat."

"Those pigs are community property."

Ingrid stood suddenly, knocking the chair over with a great clatter. "They're *our* property!" she yelled, enraged.

Harper looked at her friend standing there, naked, hands on hips, nostrils flared. "Not anymore," she said, quietly.

Ingrid retrieved her chair and sat down upon it with purpose. She folder her arms and looked away from Harper.

After a moment she got up and walked to the shelf.

Harper watched her with interest. She admired the elegant stride of Ingrid's legs, and the way the muscles undulated in her friend's buttocks. She admired once again the barbed wire tattoo on Ingrid's lower back, identical to her own, and considered how fine it still looked above Ingrid's still-perfect tush.

When Ingrid turned around, she had a big grin on her face and a huge white tub of ice cream in her arms.

"Daddy saved up a ton of ice cream for the apocalypse," Ingrid said. She pried off the lid and looked inside. She looked up again, her grin wider. "Chunky-Monkey."

"OhMyGod," Harper heard herself saying.

Ingrid brought the tub to Harper and set it down between the two chairs. She rummaged in her discarded pants pockets and produced two spoons.

"I always bring two spoons in case Kim joins me," she said. Suddenly, she looked distant, and sad. "She never does."

She handed a spoon to Harper.

They looked into the tub, then looked up at each other, each with a huge grin on their face.

They each drove a spoon into the hard ice-cream, and brought the spoons up again, with ice cream in the bowls. Their eyes glittered in anticipation.

Kim brought her spoon to Harper's mouth. Harper raised an eyebrow in surprise, then grinned and returned the gesture.

They each took the other's spoon into their mouths, and moaned with pleasure as the cold ice cream hit their palates.

The door opened and Kim entered.

She took a moment to take in the sight that greeted her, then rolled her eyes and sighed.

"I'd offer you ice cream," Ingrid said. "But I gave Harper your spoon."

Kim handed Harper a list. "This is our inventory. Of everything."

Harper took the list. "Thank you."

"Don't get ice cream on it," Kim said.

"Why don't you join us, Kim?" Ingrid said. "You deserve to cool off."

"I'm fine," she said. "Will you join us for dinner Saturday, Harper? We're killing a pig."

"Do we need Council permission to kill our own pigs?" Ingrid asked.

"You don't need Council permission as long as you're only using what you need to feed yourselves," Harper said. She stood up and handed her spoon to Ingrid, then started getting dressed.

"Why are you getting dressed?" Ingrid asked.

"I have to get going," Harper said.

"Don't go," Ingrid pouted. "I need someone to help me eat all this ice cream."

Harper turned to Kim. "I was just telling your sister that you can't feed your father to the pigs," she said. "The Council won't allow it."

They waited in silence as Harper finished dressing. As she was about to go, Kim said, "We'll figure something out."

"See that you do," Harper said, and left the freezer.

Ingrid glared at her sister. "You're always giving in to her. Do you want some ice cream?"

Kim rolled her eyes, and left her sister alone in the cold with their father's body, a tub of Chunky-Monkey ice cream, and two spoons.

Chapter Twenty-Nine

Back in the house, Kim offered Troy a glass of water, which he drank greedily.

"Don't drink too fast," Kim said. "You'll get a cramp."

Troy tried to drink more slowly.

"I just saw you out of the corner of my eye when I came in here," Kim said, "and thought you were my Dad for a second."

"Ingrid said the same thing," Troy said, between gulps. "It's because I'm wearing his clothes."

"You're a really hard worker. I appreciate that."

Troy finished drinking and wiped his mouth with his sleeve. "I want to do my part," he said.

"Yeah, well, don't we all. Except my sister."

"She wants to do her part," Troy said, gently. "She just doesn't know what that is, yet."

"Well, she better figure it out. Soon. Before they show up at our door with pitchforks and torches."

"Are they really that pissed at you?" Troy asked.

"We've always been outsiders," Kim said. "My parents were back-to-nature hippies. No one around here ever loved us. And we were pretty stuck up. My mom home-schooled us, so we didn't really get to know a lot of the other kids around here. Except Harper. Harper's a special case. Her family's lived in this valley since, I don't know, I guess since the first non-native people came here, and even before that, because she's part Native American, too. So, she's got cred, you know? And her Dad was pretty broad-minded. He was a schoolteacher, so he was educated, and raised her to be. As soon as she graduated high school, she joined the military. Did a couple of combat tours in desert shitholes. Came back and went to college on the GI Bill. Then came back here and joined her uncle in the Sherriff's department. I guess, she wanted to serve her community. Which I get now. I didn't really get that until I joined the Peace Corps. But I totally get it now. So."

She paused, unsure how to proceed, then decided to plunge right in. "You had a girlfriend?"

"Yeah," Troy said quietly. "She was in our group. We were the last two."

He paused and looked into his now empty glass.

"You don't have to talk about it," Kim said, softly.

"Remember I told you about the guys in the pick-up?" Troy said.

"The guys who stole your pants."

"She was with me when they pulled up. But when I woke up, she was gone." He paused and looked into the distance. Kim could see how haunted he was by whatever memory he was reliving. "I don't really know what I'm doing."

"What do you mean?" she asked, gently.

"I mean, should I go back and look for her?"

He looked at her and his eyes looked so lost, so stricken, Kim wanted to cry, and hold him.

"You'd never find her," she said, gently. "And if you did, they'd kill you."

"I pray every night they killed her," Troy said. "Quickly."

"I understand," Kim said.

And she did.

Chapter Thirty

Harper was in her office when Mayor Dorothea Billings walked in, in something of a tizzy.

"Harper, what happened with Henry Lowry this morning?" she demanded.

Dorothea was only a few years older than Harper. She'd taken over her aunt's job as mayor when her aunt succumbed to the first outbreak of disease from the permafrost or the tropics in the valley following the collapse. Sometimes, Dorothea seemed overwhelmed by the position. Sometimes, Harper knew exactly how she felt.

Harper very patiently explained exactly what had happened this morning.

"Harper," the Mayor said, "we can't have armed rebellion in the valley. We could be the last people on the planet for all we know. We're going to fight a civil war?"

Harper had to admit that sounded like an exceedingly bad idea. "What do you suggest?"

"Well, we can't let Lowry play by his own rules," the Mayor admitted. "And we can't go to war with him."

"So, you're asking me to make peace."

"Can you do that?"

"I'm not sure."

The Mayor looked thoughtful, hopeful, and frightened. "Can you try?"

Chapter Thirty-One

On Saturday, Kim slaughtered the pig. She made Troy go with her and help – she figured he should know how it was done. But when it came time to kill the animal, Kim did it herself. Troy looked pale – for a moment she thought he was going to faint.

They roasted the pig on a spit over an open flame. It was excessively hot. Even though it was a small pig, it took hours to roast. By the time the pig was ready, they were dripping with sweat. Ingrid, still honoring the boycott of her clothes, insisted it made more sense to do things her way in the unbearable heat – nothing, she said, felt worse than sweat soaking through clothes. Kim, however, pointed out the potential unpleasantness of one's naked body being splattered with sizzling pork drippings.

Harper showed up in her uniform and hung her gun belt on the rack in the entryway. They'd put the roasted pig in a Dutch oven to keep it warm, and everyone had managed to bathe and dress in clean clothes before she arrived. Even Ingrid, for some reason, had agreed to suspend her boycott, and appeared freshly showered, powdered, and clad in a floral sundress.

The dined on roast pork, short and slightly dry ears of corn, and canned cranberry sauce.

It was delicious.

At some point, the conversation turned to the subject of what they missed from before.

They all missed a lot. Some of what they missed was too painful to say out loud, and so no one even tried. Mostly, they tried to keep it light. But Kim felt gloomy, and spent a lot of the conversation staring into her glass of wine.

"I miss basic cable," Harper said, which was true.

"OMG!" Ingrid exclaimed in solidarity.

Encouraged, Harper said, "I miss *Naked and Afraid*."

Kim couldn't believe what she was hearing. "*Naked and Afraid*," she said, scornfully.

"I love *Naked and Afraid*!" Harper insisted.

"We could all be naked and afraid soon enough," Kim said, and drank her wine, acutely aware that, although their father's wine cellar was well stocked, eventually, this was something she would have to add to her list of things she missed.

"I'm never afraid when I'm naked," Ingrid said.

Kim rolled her eyes. "I am."

Ingrid furrowed her brow. "Why are you afraid when you're naked?"

"I'm afraid when *you're* naked, I mean."

"Why are you afraid when I'm naked?" Ingrid asked. She considered that for a moment. "You're totally lying," she declared. "No one is afraid when I am naked. Everyone is delighted. Troy, are you afraid or delighted when I'm naked?"

Aghast, Troy mumbled incoherently.

"*Naked and Delighted?*" Harper said. "Which channel was that on?" She laughed, and then so did Ingrid.

Kim had forgotten what a sweet laugh Harper had. She'd forgotten what a silly laugh Ingrid had when she wasn't laughing cruelly. God, it seemed so long ago she'd heard either one of them laugh like that. She supposed it really *was* so long ago. The trill of Harper's laugh, the irrepressible giggle of Ingrid's, Harper's big, strong teeth when she smiled – when was the last time she'd seen her smile? The way Ingrid always covered her mouth as if her laughter would drag something embarrassing out of her. It brought her back to a birthday party – was it Ingrid's? They were at the table, with Mom and Dad. So, it was before Mom had died. Ingrid had just started middle school. Kim was just finishing. Harper was in high school. They always looked up to Harper, admired her. After dinner, while Dad did the dishes, the rest of them all went skinny-dipping in the creek by the waterfall, Harper, Ingrid, Kim, and Mom. They had splashed in the cold, wonderful water, and laughed and laughed.

Mom died just before Kim went to college. Ovarian cancer. For Ingrid, it was a one-two punch, losing Mom to cancer, and then losing Kim to college. Kim knew that had been really tough on her sister. Ingrid felt like everyone had checked out on her. And then, to make matters worse, Dad really did check out, emotionally and mentally. He was lost without Mom. He grew and sold his weed, but otherwise, he just puttered around aimlessly. Ingrid basically parented herself from then on. And not always that successfully. Kim still felt kind of guilty and responsible for her.

Which is why she put up with her bullshit. Mostly.

"I hate the pixilation on *Naked and Afraid*," Ingrid cried, bringing Kim back.

"You really want to see all the gory details?" Harper asked.

"If they show us naked people," Ingrid said, "they should have the courage of their convictions and we should see naked people, not people partially clothed in pixilation. Otherwise, they're just being coy. I believe in documentary realism."

"Yeah, that's why you're stoned all the time," Kim said. "Because you love realism so much."

"Reality is for people who can't handle drugs," Ingrid said, perhaps not aware she was contradicting herself.

"Drugs are for people who can't handle you," Kim said.

"Then you should get stoned more often."

"I wish I could pixilate you."

Ingrid ignored her sister and turned back to Harper. "I miss *Chopped*," she said.

"I love *Chopped*!" Harper exclaimed.

"I miss *Say Yes to the Dress*," Ingrid added.

Harper gasped in horror. "Can you believe how much people paid for those monstrosities?"

"But Daddy wants his little girl to look like an angel, Harper!" Ingrid exclaimed.

"Gross!" Harper laughed.

"I honestly can't believe you guys," Kim said, not at all surprised Ingrid had managed to make herself the center of attention.

Harper turned to Troy. "What do you miss, Troy?"

"Baxter misses the internet," Ingrid said.

"I do miss the internet," Troy admitted.

"Sure," Ingrid said. "Where else is a guy like Baxter supposed to get his porn-fix?"

Troy turned red. Kim wondered if it was from anger or shame.

"I miss Facebook," Troy mumbled. "Um, also, my name is Troy."

"Facebook?" Ingrid said, outraged. "Facebook is for old people."

"I used to travel," Troy said, quietly. "I had friends all over the world. Facebook kept us in touch." He paused and drank some wine. "I wonder where they all are now."

That proved a bummer that brought the room down for several awkward moments.

"I don't miss anything," Kim found herself blurting out.

Ingrid looked at her like she'd just peed in the soup. "Seriously?"

"I mean, I miss Dad, but Dad would be dead even if things hadn't gone to shit," Kim said. She stared into her wine glass, visualizing the things from the world before that were no more. "I miss my friends in the Peace Corps. I hate it that so many people are dead, and that things are so scary out there." She looked up and looked everyone in the eye as they sat around the dinner table. "But in terms of our life now? We've got the house we grew up in, we've got our books, and I like working with my hands. I learned a lot growing up here and in the Peace Corps that I can use now. I mean, what was I going to do, you know? After the Peace Corps? Go to law school? Be a lawyer? Or an academic of some kind? I woke up every day and I thought about the future and it filled me with dread. Having to work some kind of stupid job for some stupid boss. I wake up every day now, and I don't think about the future. *Because there is none.* I think about the present. I think about crop rotation and irrigation and equipment maintenance. And every day will be like that -- an eternal present as far as we can see. And I am so much happier."

Kim looked at everyone at the table looking back at her with expressions of worry and pity in their eyes and wished she could disappear into her wine glass.

"You were made for the apocalypse, Kim," Harper said, quietly.

Kim downed the rest of her glass and refilled it. "Well," she said, "I do miss internet porn."

Chapter Thirty-Two

After they finished eating, they had a brief argument about whether or not to waste electricity playing music on the stereo, or if Ingrid should grace them with a song.

"Come on, Ingrid," Harper said, finally. "I want to hear you sing."

"Really?" Ingrid said. The idea seemed to take her by surprise. "Kim hates my singing."

"That is so untrue," Kim protested.

"You, on the other hand, always did like my singing, Harper," Ingrid said, smiling sweetly and, Kim thought, oddly flirtatiously.

"I still do," Harper said.

"Ok, then," Ingrid said.

They went out on the gallery and Ingrid strummed her guitar and sang "I Was Born About Ten Thousand Years Ago:"

I was born ten thousand years ago
And there's nothing in this world that I don't know
I saw Peter, Paul, and Moses playing ring around the
roses
And I'll lick the guy that says it isn't so

Ingrid knew all the verses, and she sang them all, so the song went on for a good long time. She played her final chord and let it ring out. Everyone listened to the sound echo across the valley. It seemed to echo for a long time. Ingrid wondered if they could hear it in every hollow.

"You're a really nice singer, Ingrid," Harper said, smiling.

"Elvis recorded that one in June, 1970," Troy said, awkwardly. "They used snippets of it between tracks on his 1971 album, *Elvis Country*, in '71, and the full version on *Elvis Now* in '72."

"You are a fount of useless information, Troy," Harper said. "Good thing you're not afraid to work with your hands."

Chapter Thirty-Three

Kim and Troy went in to clear the dishes while Harper and Ingrid stayed on the gallery and drank whiskey from mason jars.

"The little relief in temperature when the sun goes down makes such a difference, don't you think?" Ingrid said. "Do you think it's getting cooler at night since, you know, everything went to shit?

"I don't know," Harper said, unsure. "Maybe a little. It would be nice if we could get some rain. Might cool things down some. The soil is thirsty."

Ingrid pulled out a doobie. "Want to smoke some weed?"

Harper looked annoyed. "No, thanks."

"Mind if I smoke one?"

"I do, actually."

"Hmm," Ingrid said, feeling defiant, and fired up the doobie. "That's a shame."

She inhaled deeply and held the smoke in her lungs.

"Ingrid," Harper said with barely contained fury. "You have got to get your shit together."

Ingrid let the smoke out slowly. "I don't understand what you mean."

"Your sister is doing all the work around here."

"Well, now Baxter is helping."

"While you smoke doobies. And his name is Troy."

Ingrid gasped, struck by a horrible thought. "What do you think will happen when we run out of rolling papers? I mean, we have bongs, but I hate those."

"Ingrid!" Harper barked.

Ingrid was annoyed. "You need to take a chill pill, Harper."

"I take a chill pill, Ingrid, and people die."

"You're not responsible for the world, you know."

"I kinda am for the part of it in the valley, though," Harper said. "Which may be all there is left."

Ingrid offered her the doobie. "Seriously, you need this more than I do."

"Jesus, Ingrid, you can't go on like this," Harper said. "I know your Dad is gone and your friends at school are all probably dead and you had big plans for your future and you don't like coming back here and living with the great unwashed, but none of that matters now. We've all got to do our parts, or we are not going to make it. Including you. And people who don't pull their weight, Ingrid, the community is not going to sit by and stand for it forever. Do you know how many people want to just take over this place and take your stuff?"

"That's because they're jealous."

"People see you being your frivolous self and they get mad."

"I am not frivolous!" Ingrid protested, feeling very angry and ill-used. "I am intelligent, creative, and think outside the box."

"People need to see you getting your hands dirty, or they are going to think you are pampered and lazy."

"This isn't fair! None of this is fair!" Ingrid's voice broke and she choked back a sob. "I was supposed to be hiking the Appalachian Trail right now with my boyfriend!"

Harper softened her tone. "What's his name?"

"You mean what *was* his name," Ingrid said, trying to control the sob in her throat. "Because he's probably dead now." She took a breath. "His name was Steve."

"I'm sorry," Harper said. "Really, I am."

"Why should I feel sorry for myself?" Ingrid said, angrily. "Everyone's lost someone. Except these fucking valley hillbillies, because they don't know anyone outside the county."

"They've lost people too. When people got sick. You know that."

Ingrid pouted, then looked up at Harper. Their eyes locked.

Ingrid felt Harper's hand on the back of her neck.

Gently, Harper pulled her face to hers.

And then Harper's mouth was on her own.

Ingrid felt her heart flutter. Her mind swirled. She struggled to make sense of this.

Harper's lips felt so good on hers.

And then Ingrid was kissing back. And then their mouths were open. And tongues were involved.

Ingrid pulled back. Her heart was racing. The blood surged in her veins, filling her with excitement. Her loins tingled. "I wasn't expecting this," she admitted.

"I'm sorry," Harper said. "I don't mean to make you uncomfortable."

Ingrid realized she wasn't uncomfortable. She realized that this thing that happened, that was happening, was something that she had wanted, longed for, but never, ever realized. She didn't even know she liked girls in that way. She wasn't even sure she did.

But she was sure she liked Harper in that way.

This time, she pressed herself into Harper, and felt Harper's hands on her back, strong and certain. She pulled Harper's shirttails out of her trousers, put her hands on her chest, and began to work Harper's breasts out of her bra.

Harper hoisted up Ingrid's sundress. Ingrid was not wearing underwear – she rarely did. Harper put her hands on Ingrid's bare rump and gripped her hard, pulling her towards her, pressing their loins together.

"Is this Ok?" Harper asked.

"Shut up and sneak upstairs to my room with me," Ingrid whispered, between kisses.

Chapter Thirty-Four

They tiptoed upstairs.

Ingrid turned the latch on her bedroom door, and quickly their clothes scattered on the floor.

"Are you sure?" Harper said. "I don't want to rush you."

Ingrid's hands moved over Harper's flesh, and Harper's moved over hers. Her heart pounded and she felt breathless. "I want you to rush me," Ingrid gasped. "Please."

"Have you ever done this before?" Harper asked. "With a girl?"

"Sophomore year, I had a girlfriend for a semester," Ingrid said, as Harper kissed her neck. "But I went to Oberlin, so that was pretty much part of the curriculum. What's the best way to do this?"

Harper held her close, her hands gripping Ingrid's buttocks, Ingrid's gripping Harper's shoulders. Harper was taller than her by a bit, and she looked up into her eyes. They kissed again, and Ingrid thought their kisses were becoming more familiar and feeling really right.

"That depends what you're into," Harper said.

"I'm still figuring that out," Ingrid said, and kissed her hungrily.

"Sixty-nine works pretty well, if you're into that," Harper said.

"Please. We call it *soixante-neuf* around here," Ingrid gasped as Harper began to caress and kiss her breasts. "We are very cosmopolitan."

And then they were on the bed, and Harper's mouth was on Ingrid's sex, and Ingrid's on hers. At first Ingrid felt awkward, the intimacy almost unimaginable and a little bit embarrassing. But then she tasted Harper on her tongue and felt Harper's strong thighs in her hands and Harper's strong hands on her buttocks. Her tongue plunged deeper, feeling Harper's heat on her mouth, and she felt a pulsing surge inside of her and, soon, everything outside her bedroom was swept from her thoughts and all that remained was her and Harper and the pleasure they shared.

Chapter Thirty-Five

While Harper and Ingrid made love upstairs, Troy and Kim did the dishes in ignorance.

"Dad basically ran a marijuana empire out of here," Kim said as she washed and Troy dried. "That's why he was able to build such a nice house. He and my mom were total hippies. They wanted to live off the grid. Dad taught us a lot of self-reliance. Well, I should say he taught me. Ingrid, not so much."

"This is a hard adjustment," Troy said. "I mean, most people, they failed so hard to adjust, they died. So, I think, eventually . . . she'll adjust."

Kim looked at him. "Or die?"

"Well, probably not," Troy said. "Because she's got you."

Despite herself, Kim smiled. It was good to know Troy thought of her as resourceful enough to keep her irresponsible sister alive after the end of the world.

"What did you want to be when you grew up, Troy?" Kim asked, abruptly. It was a weird question, but it seemed weirdly apt.

"A musicologist," Troy said, not entirely convincingly.

"No, not before everything went to shit, I mean, when you were a kid."

"Oh," Troy said. "A fireman. I loved shiny red fire trucks. Still do."

"Really?" Kim said with a smile. "Maybe you can join the volunteer fire brigade. We've got a couple of water tenders -- trucks that carry their own water supply -- but I bet you know what tenders are, already. Even before things went to shit, this is a rural area, so there aren't fire hydrants everywhere. Harper keeps the tenders filled and gassed up and ready at all times. That's precious stuff, that water, almost as precious as the gasoline. We could drink that water or use it for our crops. But if there's ever a big fire in the valley, we're going to need those trucks. Do you think you'd like to do that? Be a fireman?"

"Sure," Troy said.

"You'd look cute in the uniform," Kim said, seeing the image in her mind's eye.

"You think?"

"Sure," Kim said. "Firemen are sexy."

She immediately realized she may have been too forward.

"Um," Troy stammered.

"I'm sorry," Kim said, feeling her face burn a shameful red. "I've made you uncomfortable. Forget I said it."

"I – "Troy hesitated. "I don't want to forget it."

Kim liked the sound of that.

The moment settled in, at first comfortably, and then awkwardly. Kim frantically searched her mind for something to say, finding her mind a total blank.

Then the scent caught her.

"Do you smell that?" she asked.

Chapter Thirty-Six

Kim took Troy by the hand and let him out onto the gallery. It was by now dark, only a dim glow still in the sky at the horizon. The night was a smidge cooler than the day, but just a smidge.

"Breathe deep," Kim said, closing her eyes, still holding his hand. It felt good, his hand in hers. It fit nicely.

"Oh," Troy said, surprised by the rich scent. "That's lovely."

"It's night-blooming jasmine," Kim said. "My mom planted it. Ages ago. I haven't smelled it in . . . I don't know how long. Since things started to get overheated and the ground parched. I thought the jasmine had all died. Do you think the air is getting sweeter since -- since . . . you know? Without all those cars and belching factories and shit?"

"I think it is a little, yeah," Troy said.

"I think so too. Fresh air. The upside of the collapse of industrial civilization."

They stood there a moment, inhaling the scent of the jasmine. Kim still held Troy's hand. They stood close together.

And then it happened. They turned to one another, and they kissed, at first hesitantly, then with passion. Troy held her, and their hands began to move up and down one another, and then Kim had her hand inside Troy's shirt, feeling his bare back on her fingers, and Troy did the same, his hand on her lower back, the other on her bare shoulder blade. She felt him start to swell inside his pants, and her body began to tingle in anticipation. She put her hand to his crotch, feeling the outline of his hardness. She unbuckled his pants, and put her hand inside, taking his erection in her fist. He hoisted up her sundress and put his hand down her underwear and touched her sex, caressing her, and right away she felt her loins fill with heat.

And then Troy broke away.

"I -- I'm sorry," he stammered, fumbling to button his pants. "I can't."

"It's Ok," Kim said, disappointed, but trying not to let it show. She adjusted her underwear and smoothed out her sundress. "I know. Your girlfriend. Too soon. Too raw. I understand." And she did understand. She really did. "It's Ok. Really. I get it."

"I just . . . I don't know what I'm going to do."

"I know," Kim said, softly. "To fill that hole in your heart. That ball of pain and emptiness in your gut. I know. I've been there."

Troy looked at her. His eyes were moist. "Yeah?"

Kim took a breath. Then she said it.

She told him about Neil.

Chapter Thirty-Seven

"I had a boyfriend," she explained. "Neil. In the Peace Corps. In West Africa. When I came home to help take care of Dad, he stayed in Africa. We kept in touch with e-mail and skype and Facetime and stuff. Things went to shit there before they went to shit here. So, I got to see it happen to him, before it happened to us. Remember earlier when I said I didn't miss anything from before everything went to shit? I lied. I miss the fuck out of Neil." She paused, and looked at her feet, not sure if she could go on. Then, she looked Troy hard in the eye, with determination. "The last thing he said to me before the power went out on his phone was 'tell everyone I was brave.'" Kim paused again, for a long time. When she spoke again, her voice cracked, barely above a whisper, as she felt the emotion well in her chest. "And he was, too. He was really brave."

Kim felt like she was going to break down and sob. She hadn't felt these feelings since it had happened. Things had been moving too fast.

"God, I -- I'm so sorry," Troy said. "Here I am thinking I'm the only one suffering."

"No, please, don't feel that way," Kim assured him, wiping away a tear with her sleeve. "We're all entitled to our grief. We don't have to apologize for it." Kim looked out at the darkened sky. "I'm sorry I pushed. With the kissing and groping and everything."

"You didn't push."

"It's Ok. Whatever happens, Troy. One way or another.

It'll be Ok."

Troy looked at her. Kim returned his gaze. He looked at her like he thought she was nuts.

"How can you be so sure?" he said.

Chapter Thirty-Eight

Kim was up first, as she always was. She made coffee and breakfast, and then went to wake her sister.

She found Harper snoring quietly, lying naked and face down on her sister's bed. Ingrid was nowhere to be found.

Well, that's interesting, Kim thought.

She checked the guest bedroom, but the bed hadn't been slept in.

Curiouser and curiouser, Kim thought.

She checked her watch. The sun was up, but it was still early. She decided to let everyone sleep for a moment longer while she went to find her sister. She had a feeling she knew where she was.

She was right.

She found Ingrid in the creek on their property, sitting naked on a rock in the spray of the waterfall, which was more of a trickle than the cascade it had once been.

Even though her sister was wet from the spray, Kim could tell that some of the droplets on Ingrid's face were tears.

Ingrid looked up, saw her sister, and wept harder.

Kim considered for a while what to do. Eventually, she decided to give in to her sister's silliness.

Kim stripped naked, leaving her clothes in a pile on the bank, and waded into the creek, eventually sitting beside her sister on a flat stone.

OhMyGod, she thought, as she let the water splash over her. That feels so good.

"It's all gone," Ingrid blubbered.

"What's all gone?" Kim asked.

Ingrid waved her arms. "Everything!"

"Everything?"

"The entire creek is gone!"

Kim looked around. "Ingrid, what do you think that stuff is your feet are soaking in?"

"The water used to be up to our necks! Don't you remember when we used to swim here?"

It was true the water was just deep enough in which to wade now. Still, it ran clear and cool.

"Put your head back," Kim commanded her sister.

Ingrid looked at her, perplexed, then closed her eyes and did as she was told, letting the water fall onto her face.

"Open your mouth," Kim said. "Drink."

Ingrid opened her mouth and let it fill with water, then sat upright again, and swallowed.

"How's it taste?" Kim asked.

Ingrid coughed a little, but managed to sputter out, "OhMyGod, it's wonderful."

Kim smiled and put her hand on her sister's shoulder. "We are so lucky, Ingrid. We have good, clean water to drink and to bathe in." She pointed, vaguely into the distance. "That's more than almost anywhere else outside the valley."

Ingrid looked at her, and blinked, eyes wide, eyelashes drooping with tears, her nose running, her cheeks flushed.

Then she put her head on Kim's shoulder and cried.

Kim held her in her arms until the crying stopped.

Chapter Thirty-Nine

Harper drove up to the Lowry compound with a bottle of Johnny Walker Blue that cost her a month of honey jars to procure.

She was met by a dozen angry looking armed men. She took a breath and climbed out of the Crown Vic, one hand on the grip of her sidearm, the other on the neck of the bottle.

Lowry, standing on the gallery of his house, a ramshackle 19th century farmhouse built by his grandfather, beckoned for her to join him.

"Peace offering?" he said, as she offered him the bottle.

"Why don't you and I see if we can iron a few things out?" Harper suggested.

Lowry looked at the bottle, then looked back at Harper. "I'll go get a couple of glasses."

They sat in the shade of the gallery at a wooden table and sipped the Scotch.

"I'm going to evict the residents of the Piney Woods Trailer Park," Lowry announced. "They haven't paid me rent since the collapse."

Harper gritted her teeth and struggled not to blurt out, simply, *no you're not.*

"Henry," she said. "You know the Council has ordered the suspension of all evictions pending further notice."

Lowry swirled around the amber liquid in his glass,

staring at it. "On what authority?"

"On the authority of the emergency measures enacted by the Council at the onset of the crisis."

Lowry looked at her across his glass. "It's not a crisis anymore, Sheriff. This is the status quo now. It won't pass. It's permanent. How much longer is the Council going to use this as an excuse for an unprecedented power-grab?"

"Ok, look," Harper said. "You need to take your concerns up with the Council. In the meantime, my job is to uphold order and the law."

"The Council follows your lead, Harper. You're both legislator and enforcer."

"The question on the table, Henry, is how can we work together to avoid conflict?"

"You can stay out of my way and let me attend to my interests as I see fit."

"That's not going to work if you're illegally evicting people and damming the water supply."

Lowry downed his drink in one gulp. "Thank you for the drink, Sheriff. It's been nice visiting with you."

"Henry."

"I think you know the way out."

Harper paused and stared at Henry, who looked back at her, implacable.

"You have that inventory for me, Henry?" she asked.

Henry ignored the question. "Good day to you Sheriff. God speed."

"In one week, Henry. I'm coming for that inventory."

"Safe travels to you."

Harper decided to take her leave before her anger made her say something impolitic.

That went well, she thought, as she climbed into the Crown Vic and turned the ignition.

Chapter Forty

To Kim's surprise, Ingrid joined them in the field mid-morning.

Kim had to send her back to put on long sleeves and pants and a hat. To her further surprise, Ingrid returned, this time properly outfitted for a day of work.

Ingrid was slow, but she didn't complain. That is, not until they returned to the house to escape the heat of mid-day and eat some lunch.

"OhMyGod," Ingrid cried, as she plopped down in the shade of the gallery and Kim handed her a cup of water. "This is what they do to political prisoners in China."

"Used to do," Troy said between gulps of his own water. "They probably ate them all. By now."

Kim was a little horrified to hear this. "They ate the Chinese political prisoners? Who did?"

"Other Chinese?" Troy said, uncertainly. "Is that racist?"

Kim wasn't sure. "Is it?"

"Well, I mean, they used to harvest their organs and stuff," Troy explained. "So, I wouldn't put it past the Red Army to resort to cannibalism at a time like this. But, I mean, that's strictly a political critique, not a cultural or ethnic one."

Ingrid, meanwhile, had been pouring herself glass after glass of water and downing each one.

Annoyed and concerned, Kim took the pitcher away.

"OhMyGod, it is so fucking hot!" Ingrid exclaimed. "That

sun is relentless! The humidity is like a perspiration beast living on your skin and sitting on your chest! I am absolutely going to die here!"

Kim was irritated. "See, actually, you're not. That's the kind of thing we used to say when actually just dropping dead was a totally remote possibility. But, now, since it's not, 'I am absolutely going to die here' is the kind of thing that people might actually take seriously, so you shouldn't say it anymore unless it's actually true."

"OhMyGod, will you shut up?" Ingrid exclaimed, her faced flushed, her hair matted to her scalp with sweat. "I am absolutely going to plotz! Can I say that! 'Plotz?' Or has the apocalypse made 'plotzing' politically incorrect, too?"

Kim was so angry at her whiny sister at this point she didn't want to say anything for fear she'd say something she'd regret.

"I think it's probably Ok if you say 'plotz,'" Troy said, adding, sheepishly, "just my two cents."

"Yeah," Kim grumbled. "I think 'plotz' is Ok."

"Is anyone going to make any fucking lunch?" Ingrid demanded.

Kim looked at her angrily. "Actually, it's your turn."

"You're kidding, right?" Ingrid said.

"We have a schedule."

"Your ass has a schedule. Jesus H. Is this our life now? Backbreaking labor in the sun, communal ownership of our land, livestock, and property, Council dictates regarding the allocation of our resources, and only a tiny plot of land for weed cultivation? Living like fucking kulaks under Stalin's five-year plan? And on top of that, there's no one to make me my fucking lunch?"

"There's you," Kim said, evenly. "There's you to make you your fucking lunch."

"I hate my life!" Ingrid said.

"There's nice things, too," Troy blurted out.

Ingrid had her doubts. "Name one!"

"You can still watch DVDs."

Ingrid thought that over. It was a revelation. "You're

right. Baxter's right."

Troy corrected her. "Troy."

"With Brad Pitt? No, I hate that movie," Ingrid said. "*Troy* sucks." She turned to her sister. "Baxter's right. Why don't we watch DVDs anymore?"

"Because," Kim explained patiently for the one millionth time, "it would be really shitty for us to be up here watching DVDs at night while the rest of the valley is sitting in the dark."

"First of all, who gives a shit about the rest of the valley, it's not our fault they didn't prepare, and anyway, who is even aware of what we're doing up here?"

"They can see the lights burning up here, when all around the rest of the valley is mostly darkness."

"Well, fuck them. I want to watch a DVD! I only wish Dad had bought a Blu-Ray before he got sick."

"It's your turn to make lunch," Kim reminded her.

"It's your ass's turn to make lunch!" Ingrid exclaimed.

With a howl of protest, Ingrid stood up, farted, and stomped into the house.

Kim hoped she was going to make lunch.

Chapter Forty-One

Harper picked up Daryl and took him to her place for lunch.

"We need to break up," Harper blurted out over turkey sandwiches.

"Oh," Daryl said, looking surprised and a little bit hurt.

"I'm seeing someone else."

"I'm Ok with that," Daryl assured her.

"No, what I mean is – "

"You're seeing someone who makes you not want to see anyone else?" Daryl asked.

Harper smiled. Daryl could sometimes show remarkable sensitivity, she thought. She'd miss him. But she felt certain of this.

"Yes," Harper said. "That's exactly what I mean."

Daryl put down his sandwich.

"Can we do something first?" he asked.

Harper wasn't sure what he was going to ask, but he looked so adorable and hopeful that she thought to herself that she was likely to accommodate him if at all possible.

Ten minutes later, Harper stood in the bathroom, regarding herself in the mirror with skepticism.

"You ready?" Daryl called from her bedroom.

Harper wasn't at all sure that she was. She took a deep breath, and stepped into the bedroom, wearing her sheriff's hat, her gun-belt, cowboy boots, and nothing else.

Daryl regarded her with delight from her bed. He lay naked, his erection standing tall, quivering in anticipation. Harper thought he looked sexy like that. Not as sexy as Ingrid, but sexy, nonetheless.

Daryl brought a Polaroid camera up and it flashed, momentarily blinding her.

"Where did you get that?" Harper asked, as the camera spat out the picture.

"In your bureau," Daryl said, innocently.

"What were you doing snooping in my drawer?"

"Looking for this," Daryl said, with his shit-eating good-ol' boy grin that most of the women in the valley, including Harper, found irresistible.

"Do you know how much that cost me?" Harper said. "Six mason jars of honey."

"Funny how something that was an outdated piece of junk is now a precious commodity, since there's no electricity," Daryl said, waving the picture in the air to assist the drying process. He regarded it with interest. "A little faded, 'cause the film's so old, but not bad." He looked at her. "Strike a pose or something, ok?"

Harper tilted her hat, put one hand on the brim, another on the butt of her gun, and shifted her weight to one leg, and bent the other at the knee. "How's this?"

"Perfect," Daryl said, and snapped another photo. "now, same pose, if you please, Mademoiselle Sheriff, but turn around and look at the camera over your shoulder."

Harper felt self-conscious and panicked. "Oh, I don't know about that," Harper said.

"Why not?" Daryl pouted

"You know why not."

"You should not be self-conscious about your butt, Harper," Daryl said with such conviction, she almost believed him.

She turned around and struck the pose. The camera flashed.

"These pictures stay here," Harper insisted. "No way are you taking them with you."

"Can I come over and look at them from time to time?"

Harper laughed. "We'll see about that."

"Now," Daryl requested, "let's strike a couple poses with your gun drawn."

They made love, Harper straddling his loins, facing away from him, in the "reverse cowgirl" position. Daryl asked her to wear the hat, gun-belt, and cowboy boots as they made love, and Harper agreed. But she did holster her sidearm.

Harper saw a flash and heard the Polaroid whirl as it spat out another photo.

"My ass better look good in that shot," Harper said.

"Your ass looks great all the time," Daryl assured her.

Harper adjusted herself to face Daryl, straddling his loins again, guiding him inside her. She figured, if this was going to be their last time, he wanted to look into her handsome face, for a change.

Daryl took another photo.

"You're the best cowgirl, ever," Daryl said.

Harper felt a surge of pleasure, and threw back her head and closed her eyes, hearing the whirl of the camera and seeing its flash through her lids as she did.

Chapter Forty-Two

To Kim's surprise and delight, after about fifteen minutes, Ingrid returned with a platter of sandwiches.

"Lunch is served, motherfuckers," Ingrid said. "I made Reuben sandwiches."

"Really?" Kim said. She was sort of amazed.

Ingrid put her platter down and gestured expansively as she explained. "We don't have kraut, but we do have cabbage, and we don't have Swiss, but we do have that goat cheese Dad taught us to make, and we don't have rye, but we do have that thick good black bread you baked the other day, and we don't have Russian dressing, but we do have that crazy delicious mustard that Harper's mom gave us, and we don't have corned beef, but we do have that pork left over from dinner the other day."

"So, basically, you made ham sandwiches," Kim said.

"Your ass made ham sandwiches," Ingrid said. "I made Reubens, with improvised ingredients."

Kim grabbed a sandwich and took a bite. "OMG, this is delicious," she said, mouth full.

"I know, right?" Ingrid said.

Kim turned to Troy. "You have to try this. It tastes nothing like a Reuben, but it is delicious."

Troy took a bite and moaned appreciatively.

"I got the cheese to be all melty because we still have electricity," Ingrid said, proudly.

They ate in silent appreciation for a long time.

When they were finished, they sat back and allowed themselves time to digest before the inevitable return to the fields.

"So," Ingrid said. "This is our life, now."

Kim nodded, solemnly. "I guess," she said. "Pretty much. I guess it is."

Chapter Forty-Three

It was night, and Harper was on patrol.

The radio squawked and Dawkins, sounding panicked, said that Harper needed to get down to the checkpoint.

Harper rushed down to the entrance to the valley in the Crown Vic, screeched to a stop, and went to Dawkins and Percy, standing behind the trucks they parked diagonally to block the road, their guns drawn. Half a dozen more deputies crouched nearby, their guns drawn as well, aimed into the darkness of the road.

Harper remembered when the road was lighted by lamps. But now it was only blackness.

"What is it?" Harper asked.

"Someone's out there," Dawkins said. "Someone's coming."

"Why do you say that?"

"We heard them."

Harper listened.

She heard an owl. She heard cicadas. She heard the peep of the tree frogs. The night was so much louder now that it wasn't drowned out by humanity.

And then she heard the sound of an engine revving.

"Brace yourselves," Harper said, as she slung the carbine off her shoulder and took aim into the night.

The sound grew louder and the vehicle grew closer, but they could not see it in the darkness until it was almost upon them. It came out of the black, headlights off, screeched to a halt, and then shots rang out.

Dawkins was thrown off his feet, a slug smashing his shoulder.

Shit, Harper thought, and fired.

Muzzle flashes lit the night. She could hear bullets zip by. It took her right back to Iraq.

Harper aimed at the muzzle flashes and fired again. She heard someone cry out. She aimed again.

A man appeared out of the darkness, running to her with a rifle, a bayonet affixed to the barrel.

A fucking bayonet? Harper thought.

Harper fired and took off the top of his head

The man fell, as a second man appeared, grabbing the rifle from his dead comrade's hands and continuing the charge.

The man was upon her before she could fire again, leaping to the blockade truck's hood and thrusting the bayonet at her chest.

Harper fell back and rolled away, feeling the blade slice through her uniform and cut the flesh at her shoulder. It wasn't deep, but it hurt. She stumbled to her feet; the man was still coming at her. He thrust. Harper leaped to the side. The blade grazed the flesh at her rib cage. Her carbine lay on the cracked asphalt. She fumbled for her sidearm. The man swung his rifle in a wide arc. The edge of the bayonet cut through her uniform and sliced the skin of her belly. The man jabbed at her again, grazing her chest. Harper had the sidearm out and was taking aim, but the man swung again. She dodged, but the blade scraped the back of her hand and her weapon dropped.

Fuck this shit, she thought, and she grabbed the rifle's barrel and thrust it up and backwards, twisting it out of the man's hands, and jabbing the end of the bayonet through the man's throat.

The man sat down hard on the road, his fingers weakly grasping the blade that stuck through the front of his throat and protruded out the back of his neck. He gurgled and fell over on his side.

Harper scrambled for her sidearm, came up in a kneeling

position, held her weapon two-handed, and squeezed off a round that took off another intruder's jaw.

There was almost a dozen of them converging on four of her deputies. Two of her men were down, and the remaining two were visibly bleeding.

The intruders carried a variety of weapons, including axes and baseball bats. But only one seemed to carry a working pistol.

Harper took out the one with the pistol first, landing a shot in his chest and knocking him off his feet. She took out two more, and her deputies seemed to rally, firing volley after volley, as she fired with them, and the intruders went down one by one.

Those remaining on their feet suddenly broke off and ran for their vehicle, a rusted old pick-up truck. Harper ordered her men to keep firing. They hit at least two of the men as they ran, but only one went down. By her count, half a dozen made it to the truck. The driver gunned the truck in reverse. Harper ejected a clip, jammed in another, pulled back the receiver, sliding a round into the chamber, and fired round after round at the receding pick-up. Its tires blew and it continued in reverse as the rims shredded the rubber. Harper took aim and put a bullet through the windshield. Blood splattered the interior of the cab and the truck rolled to a halt. Five men tumbled from the truck. One of them, Harper thought, had something that looked like one of those backpacker guitars slung on his shoulder.

Harper fired after them as they disappeared into the night.

Chapter Forty-Four

Harper was bleeding through her uniform when she showed up at Ingrid and Kim's place. She surprised them on the gallery, where Ingrid was strumming her guitar while Troy and Kim listened.

"Oh my God, what happened?" Ingrid said.

Harper began to explain, but Kim instructed Troy to go into the house and come back with cotton swabs, hot water, and iodine. Then she told Harper to undress.

Harper thought of protesting, but instead, she stripped off her uniform.

"Your underthings too," Kim said.

Harper took everything off.

"Jesus," Kim said. "You're bleeding."

Troy returned. Harper was too tired to care that she was standing naked in front of him.

As Ingrid and Kim wiped away the blood and applied iodine to her wounds, Harper explained what had happened.

"Jesus Christ, Harper," Kim said in wonder as she cleaned the wound on the Sheriff's belly. "You should have Doc Wilson take a look at you."

"Doc Wilson's got his hands full with people with actual bullet holes in them," Harper said, wincing in pain.

"Are you sure you're not shot?" Ingrid asked. Kim thought she sounded panicked.

"I'm not shot. These are bayonet wounds."

"Oh, fuck," Ingrid said. "Bayonets?"

"I can't tell if any of the wounds are deep," Kim said.

"None of them are deep," Harper said. "They're superficial. It's not my first time in a firefight. It's not my first time hand-to-hand, either. I'd know if they were deep."

"What happened to the guys in the truck?" Kim asked.

"There's ten bodies lying in the Bradcock Funeral home now," Harper said. "The rest we chased back past the checkpoint. I think I've got seven deputies wounded in some way or another, some worse than others. None dead. So far. I've had fifty cals from the armory mounted at both checkpoints in and out of the valley, and I've doubled the guard and the patrols. Still, our guys are mostly farm boys. Only a few of them have military or law enforcement experience."

Kim noticed Troy standing quietly nearby. "Troy, go inside for a minute, ok? Give Harper some privacy."

But Troy stood his ground.

"Was there a woman with them?" Troy blurted out. "The guys in the pick-up truck? Did they have a woman with them? Wearing, like, a shark-tooth pendant?"

Harper looked at him with concern. "There was no woman with them. They were all men."

"Did one of them have a backpacker guitar?" Troy asked. "One of those skinny ones you carry on your back?"

This worried Harper. "One of them did, actually. At first, I thought it was a shotgun in a scabbard. He escaped back past the checkpoint."

"Ok," Troy said, and started to walk back in the house.

"Troy, stay," Harper said. "You might as well hear this."

Chapter Forty-Five

Harper didn't care about her nakedness, anymore. Modesty was a luxury she could not afford. After the end of the world, it was necessary to prioritize.

"Do you guys have weapons?" Harper asked.

"Weapons?" Ingrid repeated with alarm.

"Dad had a few shotguns and a few deer rifles," Kim said. "About a dozen hand guns, and a vintage Winchester."

"The Winchester actually fire?" Harper asked.

"Yeah, it fires pretty good, actually," Kim said.

"Dad never took me shooting," Ingrid grumbled. "He always took you."

"You had other interests," Kim said.

"I'd have been interested if he ever asked."

Kim couldn't believe they were having this conversation. No matter how extreme the situation, the same old sibling rivalry always reared its head. "Dad taught you to play guitar. He never taught me that. He taught us different things."

"You all need to carry a weapon on your person every time you leave the house from now on," Harper interrupted. "Even when working the fields. And keep one nearby when you're indoors as well."

"Oh, Jesus," Ingrid said. Kim thought maybe at long last she was getting her head around the gravity of the situation.

"These guys are coming back," Harper said, gravely.

"Guaranteed. Maybe with more guys, or maybe with just the guys who got away, maybe that was all of them. But either way, if they can't force their way through the checkpoints, they'll try coming over the mountains."

"That's impossible," Ingrid insisted. "There's no way in or out of the valley except the main road."

"There's the old trails," Kim reminded her.

"There's no way anyone who doesn't know the terrain around here can find those," Ingrid said.

"You don't want to be caught without a weapon if it turns out there is," Harper said.

"So, this is, what?" Ingrid said. "Our Second Amendment solution?"

"There's no Second Amendment anymore, Ingrid. There's only us."

They were silent as Kim walked around Harper, examining her wounds, making sure the bleeding had stopped. Troy slipped back inside the house.

"I'm going to leave you guys a radio," Harper said. "You need me, you can reach me at the Sherriff's office or in my patrol car."

"We need to let the iodine dry before we put on the bandages," Kim said. "Don't put on your clothes yet, they'll stain."

"My clothes are already stained," Harper pointed out. "Blood stains."

"Let yourself air dry for a few minutes," Kim said.

"I feel stupid just standing here like this," Harper said, and suddenly laughed awkwardly in embarrassment, her discomfort in her nakedness returning.

"Shut up," Kim said. "You're among friends."

"Stay here tonight," Ingrid said.

"I have to get back to my deputies. I'm going to need to bring Doc Wilson some of your antibiotics, too. That's the reason I came out here, actually."

"What about all that shit you took from the pharmacies?" Ingrid said, suddenly irritable.

"We used a lot of that when the sickness hit the valley,

and we need to save every dose we can for the next one," Harper explained.

"How many do you need?" Kim said.

"About a thousand doses, to be safe," Harper said.

"A thousand?" Ingrid repeated, outraged.

"I've got men with bullet holes in them," Harper spat, her voice harsher than Kim had ever heard it. "Your neighbors."

"Not *my* neighbors," Ingrid insisted.

"Men who risked everything to protect you and your sister up here in your palace of light.," Harper said.

"I never asked for their protection," Ingrid said, petulantly.

"No," Harper said, her voice barely above a whisper. "You didn't have to. Because they provided it, anyway."

"I'll get you two thousand doses," Kim said. "Make sure you take a couple yourself. You don't know where that bayonet had been. Does Doc Wilson have tetanus shots? We do, if you're not up to date with your shots. We also have tetanus antitoxin doses. Have a drink with us before you go. While the antiseptic dries."

Harper hesitated. "One drink," she conceded.

Ingrid poured glasses of whiskey and handed them out.

Troy came out from the house then, as naked as the day he had arrived, if less hirsute.

Chapter Forty-Six

Everyone stared in perplexity at Troy for a moment as he stood there in his nakedness.

Then Ingrid handed him a drink.

"Thanks," Troy said, taking the drink. "For everything. I want to thank you guys. For everything."

"Troy, what's going on?" Kim asked, concerned.

"I'm leaving."

"Without your clothes?" Harper asked.

"They're not my clothes," Troy pointed out.

"You can keep the clothes, for fuck's sake," Kim said, agitated. "Why are you leaving? Where're you going?"

"I'm going to find her," Troy said.

"Troy," Harper said.

"Those guys in the pick-up truck," Troy said.

"You don't know it was the same guys."

"Yeah, I do," Troy said. "How many pick-up trucks are out on the road outside the valley these days? There's no gas. Chances are it's them. And they're still in the area. And they're on foot, now. I can catch up with them."

"These are dangerous men," Harper pointed out.

"You've cut their number at least in half. Thanks for doing that, by the way. And at least some of the survivors are likely wounded. If I'm ever going to find out what happened to her, this is my best shot."

"You'll get killed," Ingrid said.

"I have to try," Troy said.

"Troy," Kim said, feeling her voice crack. "We need you here."

Troy turned to her and looked her in the eye with regret and affection. "I can't thank you enough for taking me in."

"We didn't just take you in. You're a part of this place now." Kim paused. "A part of the family."

"Well, I wouldn't say a part of the family," Ingrid interjected.

"I need you to help maintain this place," Kim said.

"I'll be back, if I can," Troy said.

"You won't be back," Harper corrected him. "If you do this."

"I have to know," Troy said.

Harper sighed. "At least look at the truck. It's near the checkpoint. Make sure it's the same one. There's some bodies in the morgue. See if it's the same guys. Will you do that?"

"I didn't really get a good look at anyone when they attacked us on the road," Troy said. "But, yeah. Sure. I'll do that."

"Take a shotgun," Kim said.

"I don't know how to shoot."

"It's easy," Kim said. "I'll show you."

"You guys might need that shotgun," Troy said.

"Take it."

"Ok," Troy said softly.

They stood there, awkwardly, Harper and Troy in their nakedness, glasses of whiskey in hand, everyone wanting a drink, no one knowing whether to just drink, or raise a toast, and if so, to what?

Ingrid, on a whim, picked up her guitar and sang:

Stop God almighty let me tell you the news
My head's been wet with the midnight dews
Coming down on my bended knees
Talking to the man from Galilee

My God spoke and he spoke so sweet
I thought I heard the shuffle of angel's feet
He put one hand upon my head
Great God almighty let me tell you what he said:

Go tell that long-tongued liar, oh well well
Go tell that midnight rider, oh well well
Tell the gambler, rambler, back-biter
Tell them God almighty gonna cut them down

Run on for a long time,
Run on for a long time,
Let me tell you God almighty gonna cut you down

As usual, Ingrid knew all the many verses, and she made sure to sing them all. The song went on for a while. At a certain point, Harper felt the iodine was dry enough, but she opted to wait until the song was over before getting dressed. The night air felt good on her bare skin.

Ingrid finished the song. The last chord rang out and faded into the night.

Troy raised his glass.

"To the future," he said.

Everyone looked at him like he was insane, but they raised their glasses too, and everyone drank deeply.

Chapter Forty-Seven

Harper returned to the clinic with the antibiotics. She stayed the night, dozing in a chair in the waiting room, waiting to make sure all of her men would pull through.

In the morning, assured, she went back to her house, walked to the upstairs bathroom, and turned on the taps to take a cold shower.

Water trickled from the pipes and then went dry.

Shitmotherfuckingsonofabitch, Harper thought.

Harper arrived at the pumping station by the reservoir with Percy, one of her less experienced deputies, as backup. With so many of her staff recovering from their wounds or manning the checkpoints, she had to make do.

She was greeted by a dozen armed men, Lowry among them.

"What do we do?" whispered Percy.

"Stay in the Crown Vic," Harper said. "If shooting starts, high tail it out of here and head straight for one of the checkpoints and report what happened."

"What about you?" Percy asked.

"I'll either be beside you in the car," Harper said, "or I won't. Either way, you get to a checkpoint, with or without me."

Harper climbed out of the Crown Vic.

"Henry," she said, as friendly as possible. "Am I going to have to ask for that bottle of Scotch back?"

"That won't be necessary," Lowry said. "We can turn the valves back on easy enough."

"Well, I'd appreciate it if you did that," Harper said, "given that this is city property and you have no right to be here."

Lowry gestured to the men around him. "I've got twelve guns to your one," he said. "Two if you count young Percy there, which is a dubious proposition at best. That gives me the right to be here."

"That's what you think, is it?" Harper regarded Lowry with her eyes narrowed, trying to suss him out. She could see he was taken aback by her confidence, her apparent disregard for his superiority in numbers and arms. He was trying to figure out if she was bluffing. She was trying to figure out the same thing about him.

Harper decided Lowry wasn't bluffing. She had to make sure he understood that she wasn't either.

"I want the restoration of my property rights," Lowry said. "I'm going to maintain the occupation of the pumping station, to make sure that happens."

"I didn't ask you what you wanted, Henry," Harper said, trying to maintain an even tone and not let the adrenal rage surging through her bring a quaver to her voice. "You need to vacate these premises post haste. End of discussion."

"You'll get the water flowing again once we have an agreement," Lowry said. "Property rights and propane. Take it to the Council if you want. I can wait a long time. The people with their water cut off, you ask them how long they think they can wait."

Harper thought she detected a note of doubt in Lowry's voice.

As she got back into the Crown Vic, she hoped she was right.

Chapter Forty-Eight

Kim spent most of the day training Troy in the use of firearms, and training Ingrid in the use of the Winchester. Then they outfitted Troy with as many provisions as he could carry, as well as a cut-down pump-action with a pistol grip in a side scabbard ("not even a little bit street-legal," Kim explained), and a pistol.

He left at sundown.

Kim and Ingrid sat in silence sipping whiskey as the sky darkened and the air cooled off slightly with the night.

"I'm worried about Troy," Kim admitted. "Do you think he's all right?"

"Honestly?" Ingrid said. "I think he's probably dead, or will be soon."

"Well," Kim said, trying not to show her fear and sorrow. "That's too bad."

"Yeah," Ingrid agreed. "He had a pretty good singing voice. He should have stayed."

"Do you think there's any sense to it?" Kim asked. "Troy going after his girlfriend?"

"Very little," Ingrid said.

"What if it was you or me? Or Dad? What if the only way to know if one of us were alive or dead or kidnapped or suffering was to take a risk like that? What would we do?"

"I don't know. What would you do?"

"I don't know." Kim sipped her whiskey. She stared into the valley, the shadows elongating as night fell hard. "I think I'd go after you."

Ingrid turned to her with a look of shock and delight. "Really?"

"Why is that so surprising?"

"You hate me."

"I do not hate you," Kim said. "I love you."

"I annoy the shit out of you."

"You do annoy the shit out of me," Kim admitted. "That's not the same thing as hating you. You're my sister. You're the only one I've got."

Ingrid seemed to think that over. "What about Dad? Would you go after Dad?"

Kim was surprised by her own answer. "No," she said. "Dad could take care of himself."

Ingrid didn't understand. "We both came back so he wouldn't die alone."

"That's different. That was before everything went to shit."

"So, you wouldn't risk it after everything went to shit?"

"Risking everything to be with him so he wouldn't die alone? No. He'd be dead either way."

"Wow," Ingrid said. "That's cold." She sipped her whiskey. "I wouldn't go after you, either."

Kim couldn't tell if she was serious. "No?"

"No. I'd wait for you to find me."

"What if I couldn't?"

Ingrid smiled. "You would. You accomplish everything you put your mind to. You always have."

In spite of everything, Kim smiled as well.

Chapter Forty-Nine

Judging by the look on his face, Lowry clearly hadn't expected Harper to return with Daryl's pick-up truck, Percy manning the Browning fifty caliber mounted in the rear.

It made her nervous to take the fifty cal from one of the checkpoints, but the way she figured it, keeping the water flowing was an equally urgent priority.

Harper exited the truck and strode up to Lowry in the gloaming, her hand on the butt of her gun.

"Harper," Lowry said, "you looking for a shootout here?"

By way of an answer, Harper quick-drew her sidearm and brought the barrel down across Lowry's skull in one swift motion. Lowry's eyes lost focus, and Harper grabbed him and spun him around, held him in a choke hold, and put the barrel of her gun to his temple.

His men raised their weapons, but Harper could see the uncertainty in their eyes. They glanced desperately towards one another, looking for a sign from someone for what to do.

That was when Harper heard the burst of the fifty cal.

That hadn't been part of the plan. Percy must have panicked. But it was effective, nonetheless.

The tree branches and brown, desiccated leaves above them shredded as the fifty caliber bullets tore them apart. Wood chips and bits of leaves scattered on the heads of Lowry's men as they hit the dirt.

Harper glanced at Percy, who was clearly as shocked by the burst of fire from the Browning as anyone.

"Percy," she said, *sotto voce.* "Finger outside the trigger guard, please."

Percy looked down at his finger, surprised to see it resting on the trigger. He moved his finger outside the guard.

"Gentlemen," Harper called. "Please vacate the premises immediately."

Chapter Fifty

The next morning as they sat down for breakfast (eggs and bacon and coffee), Ingrid blurted out, "Harper and I are, um, dating by the way."

Kim looked at her over her cup of coffee. "I know," she said.

Ingrid looked amazed. "How do you know?"

"You think I'm stupid?"

"No, but I didn't think you were clairvoyant."

"The first night she stayed over, I found her snoring naked in your bed."

Ingrid seemed concerned by that. "Why are you monitoring my bed?"

"I monitor everything around here. Besides, every other time she's stayed over recently, the guest bedroom is never slept in."

"How do you know I didn't give her my bed and sleep on the gallery?"

"Because I wake up at least twice a night and walk through the house to make sure everything's ok, so I'd know."

Ingrid sipped her coffee. She had switched to decaf, and didn't like it one bit. "Do you hear us?"

"Hear you?"

"You know. *Doing* it."

Kim took a big gulp of her own coffee trying to buy time to think of the right answer. "No," she said.

Ingrid was mortified. "You totally hear us."

"I don't listen at the door or anything."

"OMG."

"You guys aren't really that quiet, you know."

Ingrid turned red. "I am so embarrassed."

"Don't be." Kim smiled. "You guys are a good couple."

"We're a ridiculous couple," Ingrid said, through a mouthful of bacon.

"No, not at all. Why do you say that?"

"She's all competent, and I'm all flighty."

"That's why you work, I think. You balance each other out." Kim dipped her bacon in her egg yolk. "I mean, I did always think you liked boys."

Ingrid shrugged. "I do like boys. Still do."

"Ok," Kim said, cautiously, and bit off the egg yolk-soaked corner of her bacon.

"But I like Harper better," Ingrid said. "What about you?"

"Um, I like boys, mostly, I guess," Kim stammered. "I mean, I had a girlfriend sophomore year in college. But, I'm sure it was the same for you when you went there, Oberlin College, I mean -- pretty much everyone is a lesbian for at least a semester. Her name was Holly. She was really nice. But I guess it didn't take."

"No, I don't mean were you ever with a girl," Ingrid laughed. "I mean -- is there anyone you're into? Now?"

"Oh."

"I mean, I know you were into Troy."

"I wasn't into Troy."

"You're a liar, yes you were. But, I mean, assuming he's gone for good, are there any other prospects?"

Kim thought that over. She had an answer, but she wasn't sure she wanted to admit it. She chewed another piece of bacon, contemplatively. She sipped her coffee. She wiped her mouth.

"Quit stalling," Ingrid demanded.

"I like Daryl," Kim confessed.

Ingrid seemed shocked and delighted. "Daryl who pumps

gas?"

"He used to pump gas," Kim corrected. "There's no gas to pump anymore. Just the stuff that Harper's got under lock and key."

"I like Daryl who used to pump gas," Ingrid admitted. "He's all muscly."

Kim had to agree. "I know, right?"

"Have you ever had a conversation with him?"

Kim considered for a long time whether or not to fess up. "I danced with him at the roadhouse once," she said, finally.

"Really?" Ingrid said, her eyes widening. "When?"

Chapter Fifty-One

It was after the sisters had both come back to care for Dad, but before things had gone completely to shit. It was pretty clear that was where things were heading, if you were willing to read the signs. But most people were still in denial, and things hadn't gotten bad enough that everyone had to face the facts.

There hadn't been a delivery of anything to the valley from outside in six weeks. There were fuel shortages and food shortages and everything shortages throughout the country. Wildfires in the west. Droughts in the Midwest. Flooding in the east coast. It was on the news every day.

And it was October and it was still hot as fuck.

But the internet was still a thing and there was still electricity, even if the brownouts happened several times a day. There was still gas in Daryl's pumps, even if it was $20 a gallon. People were still getting paychecks cut and automatic deposits in their bank accounts. You couldn't get everything you wanted in the stores, and the prices were ridiculous, but no one was starving in the valley, thanks in no small part to the local farmers.

Kim had been sitting at the kitchen table skyping and then the screen went dark. She closed her laptop and sat there for a long time, a whirl of emotions roiling inside her, emotions she felt circling around a black hole in the center of her heart. She felt as if she were to allow herself to feel these feelings she'd fall into that black hole and never come out again.

So, she pushed herself away from the table. She checked on Ingrid and Dad and found them sharing a doobie on the gallery. She snuck upstairs and rummaged through her wardrobe.

When she got into the truck, checked the gage (a third of a tank), and took off for the roadhouse, she was wearing a cowboy hat, a top that exposed her shoulders, her cleavage, and her midriff, and short, short cut-off jeans that exposed just a little bit of butt crack at the top and just a little bit of both butt cheeks at the bottom. Her face was made up like a prom queen. And she wore cowboy boots.

"You never wear cowboy boots," Ingrid interrupted.

"I felt like wearing them that night," Kim said. "My legs look great in cowboy boots.

"So, this wasn't just an accidental sartorial combination. This was a look you were going for."

Kim smiled. "Oh yeah," she said. "Abso-fucking-lutely."

Kim went to the roadhouse and parked in the gravel lot. Shitkicker country music was blasting through the doors. She went inside and everyone stopped. Not all at once. A shudder of attention ran through the place, as first one, then another, noticed the little rich girl from on top of the hill, come to slum with the locals. People nudged the people next to them, who nudged the people next to them, until everyone was looking at her, some subtly, some not so much.

Kim felt the scrutiny and wanted turn back and run, but she tamped down the panic and strode to the bar. She knew she looked good, and she knew the people looking at her, judging her, knew she looked good, too. She may have looked like a slut, but so did all the other girls in the room.

The music kept blasting, so the decibel level didn't diminish that much, even though she could tell most of the conversation in the room had dropped off.

At the bar, Kim ordered a tequila. She slammed it back and ordered another.

Three tequilas in, she was feeling fine, and she was no

longer the center of attention, although a lot of people were still casting sidelong glances in her direction. She slammed back a fourth tequila, then spun on her barstool and surveyed the room, inhaling the scent of beer and cigarettes.

She saw him right away, standing across the room, wearing a wife-beater t-shirt, his muscular arms bulging, a pair of tight jeans, a big belt buckle in the center. He also had on cowboy boots, and one leg was bent at the knee as he stared at her, a bottle of beer in his hand. Kim thought at that moment he was the sexiest thing she had seen since she left the Peace Corps and came back to the valley six months ago.

Kim got up and went right for him, steady on her feet despite the tequila.

"Hi Daryl," she said. Just then, Florida-Georgia Line's "Cruise" came on the jukebox. Kim took Daryl by the hand. "Wanna dance?"

Daryl smiled one of those big good ol' boy shit-eating grins the boys 'round here were so good at, and followed her onto the dance floor.

"Did he smell like gasoline and motor oil?" Ingrid asked.

"Just enough for it to be kinda sexy," Kim said.

"What happened after you guys danced? That must have turned heads."

"The hippie kid from up the hill and the gas jockey? You bet we did."

Everybody parted to make room for them. Kim felt their eyes upon them. She didn't care.

They danced close, and then they danced closer. Feeling bold, Kim put her hands in Daryl's back pockets, and pulled him closer. Feeling permissive, she did not object when he put his hands not in her back pockets, but down inside the seat of her cut-offs. She was not wearing underwear, and his strong hands on her bare ass inside the jeans and hers on his hard butt through the pockets felt comforting. Their loins came together and grinding ensued.

Kim could feel him harden inside his jeans.

They went outside and made out in the parking lot by Daryl's pick-up. Kim unbuckled his giant buckle and undid the buttons on the front of his jeans and slipped her hand inside his pants and took him in her fist. Then, feeling reckless, she went down on him right there between his pickup and hers.

She brought him to orgasm quickly and easily. When his passion began to ebb, she got to her feet and kissed him. Daryl momentarily flinched and pulled away; then, catching himself, he brought his mouth to hers and they kissed long and hard, the hot taste of his emission on their tongues.

Kim would have preferred if he hadn't flinched, but she appreciated the effort he showed in overcoming his initial resistance and showing his appreciation with a good, long kiss.

She had to ask him to return the favor, which was a disappointment, but he smiled rakishly and promptly dropped to his knees and tugged her cut-offs down to her ankles, cupped her ass in his hands, and put his mouth to her sex. He was inelegant and lacked finesse, but he made up for it in energy and drive. Soon she found herself gripping his hair and throwing back her head and crying out as he brought her to climax.

After, he rose, and kissed her, and she did not flinch or hesitate, kissing him back hungrily, their mouths and tongues together, their tastes comingling on their tongues and lips. They clutched each other, their pants still down around their ankles, and Kim could tell he was hard again. She suggested they crawl into the cab of his pick-up truck and fuck, in exactly those terms.

And so they did. She took off her top and helped him slip out of his, so they were both naked, except for their boots. She straddled him and the drive of his loins as he thrust into her inelegantly but with purpose felt powerful, as did the muscles in his back beneath her fingers. Despite the dashboard pressing into her lower back, they brought each other to climax again.

Chapter Fifty-Two

"OMG!" Ingrid cried when Kim was finished telling her story. "That makes you practically married by valley standards. Did you use a condom?"

"We did not," Kim admitted sheepishly. "It's by the grace of God he didn't knock me up."

"OhMyGod!" Ingrid exclaimed. "I can't tell you what a relief it is to me to know you totally slutted out like that."

"Shut up!"

"I feel much better knowing I'm not the only one who can be impetuous and irresponsible. So? Is he a prospect?"

"I don't know," Kim said doubtfully but not without a modicum of hope. "He is a sweet guy, no doubt. But we don't have a hell of a lot to talk about."

"You're such a snob. There's things in life other than conversation, you know."

"Says the girl dating the smartest girl in the valley," Kim said.

"Smartest girl after you."

Kim smiled. "I'm not sure fucking Daryl in the cab of his truck was so smart."

"Did you have fun?"

"God, yes."

"Then it was smart," Ingrid assured her. "You think you guys have a future?"

"Who knows?"

"He's good stock. You know. If we're going to repopulate

the earth and everything. He's strong and healthy and has all his teeth.”

“He's not a horse, you know.”

“When this happened. You and Daryl.”

“Yeah?”

“It was right after you lost contact with Neil in West Africa, wasn't it?”

“Yeah,” Kim admitted, quietly. “Same evening, actually.”

“Shit.” Ingrid paused for a long moment, as if deciding whether or not to go on. Finally, she did. “Speaking of repopulating the earth, you should probably know something.”

“Ok.”

“I'm pregnant.”

“Oh,” Kim said. She could usually read her sister like a book, but this took her completely by surprise.

“And Daryl,” Ingrid added, “is the father.”

Chapter Fifty-Three

"Oh," Kim said. "When did this happen?"

"After Dad had passed and we had the memorial at our house. And all those people showed up and ate our food and drank our whiskey and got jealous that we still had electricity. The night before Baxter arrived."

"Troy."

"Right."

"So that's where you were all night that night."

"Yeah," Ingrid said. "I mean, getting stoned and getting laid are pretty much the only recreation available to us now, you know?"

"And it's definitely Daryl?"

"He's the only person I've had sex with in the last six months with whom I can actually procreate, so, yeah, I'm pretty sure."

"In the cab of his truck?" Kim asked.

"Not exactly."

Chapter Fifty-Four

It had happened the night after the wake, or the hillbilly shiva, whatever you wanted to call it.

Everyone was gone and Kim was asleep. Ingrid sat on the gallery amid the cigarette butts, the half-empty bottles of Dad's homemade beer, the half empty bottles of JD, and smoked a doobie. Then she smoked another.

She went down to the meat locker and stood before her father's shrouded corpse on the shelf and tried to get her mind around the idea that this lifeless shape was her Dad.

The cold of the meat locker was refreshing, but Ingrid felt like the walls were closing in on her. She left the locker and went to the front hallway. She'd kicked off her shoes earlier, and now she put on her best pair of sneakers, wondering what she would do when the sneakers wore out. Where would she get new sneakers? Would she have to wear leather shoes made from tanned animal hides like a fucking caveman or something?

She went upstairs and checked herself in the bathroom mirror. She was still wearing the black clothes she'd worn for the hillbilly shiva, and she looked good, despite her eyes which were red from crying and from weed. She reapplied some deodorant, some make-up, and tied back her hair. Then she was out the door.

It took her about an hour to walk all the way to the roadhouse, where she immediately saw Daryl in the parking lot, by his pick-up truck, drinking warm beer with his friends.

He saw her and stopped talking. He smiled at her, cautiously, but with a sideways grin that was both sexy and naughty. He approached her. He said he was sorry about her Dad. Ingrid asked him if he still had gas in his truck. Daryl said he had a little. Ingrid asked him if he had enough to drive up to the lake. He told her he did, but probably not enough to get back.

Ingrid told him that would be ok.

They climbed into his truck and in twenty minutes, they were at the lake.

There was about half the water there that used to be in the lake when they were kids. There was a long, sandy/muddy flat where once had been lake. But once you got past it, there was still water, and it was clear and lovely and deep enough to go swimming.

Ingrid stripped off her clothes and walked to the water, the mud squishing between her toes. She stepped into the water and it was still cool and refreshing. She turned back to see Daryl standing by his truck, staring at her.

"You coming in or not?" Ingrid asked.

Daryl smiled, stripped off his own clothes, and joined her in the water.

After they went skinny dipping in the lake and made their way back, Ingrid suggested they climb into the bed of his truck because she didn't want to make love on the muddy ground.

Delighted, Daryl helped her into the truck bed and climbed in after her.

Daryl lay in the bed and Ingrid straddled him, taking his erection in her hand and guiding him inside her. Daryl held her to him, his big hands on her thighs, and she undulated her hips as he thrust into her. Steadily, they brought each other to climax just as the first streaks of pre-dawn began to appear in the east.

They had to walk all the way back to town because Daryl was out of gas.

"His truck is still up there, I guess," Ingrid said. "Unless Harper appropriated it for civil defense or something."

Chapter Fifty-Five

"Does Daryl know he got you pregnant?" Kim asked.

"No," Ingrid admitted.

"Are you going to tell him?"

"I don't think so," Ingrid said. "I don't intend to raise a kid with him or anything."

"It's not a secret you can keep for long."

"Well, no one can prove it's his. There's no DNA tests anymore, and no one knows for sure how many men I've had sex with recently. You know, because I'm kind of slutty."

"Don't say that about yourself."

"That's what everyone thinks, whether or not it's true. And it's sometimes true. Even if someone canvasses every man in the valley, I don't think that'd be very scientific or anything. Weird, but not very scientific."

"Does Harper know?" Kim asked.

"Not yet," Ingrid said. "So, anyway, repopulating the earth, I mean, Daryl's guys can swim, you know? So, if that's a consideration for you -- and I guess it has to be -- he's a good prospect."

Kim wasn't sure that really made things any better. "Our kids would be both cousins and siblings," she pointed out.

"Huh." Ingrid considered. "How about that. Is that weird?"

"Yes."

"I hope this isn't going to be some kind of an impediment

to the two of you making it work."

"It is definitely going to be an impediment," Kim said.

Ingrid realized she'd fucked this up for her sister without even meaning to. This upset her. She often wanted to fuck things up for her sister, but just to annoy her – she never wanted to fuck things up irreparably.

"I'm sorry," Ingrid said.

"Well, I am too."

"Well, who knows?" Ingrid said, trying to think positively. "Maybe Troy will make it back alive after all."

Chapter Fifty-Six

Troy was out of the valley about a week when he found Lilly in a ditch on the side of the road.

She was almost unrecognizable. Her skin was mummified around her bones. Her clothes had been ripped to shreds.

There was enough of her t-shirt left for him to know it was her. Plus, there was the shark-tooth pendant around her neck.

Troy carefully took the pendent. He wanted to bury her, but he had nothing to use to dig.

He kept walking. He felt surprisingly numb. He knew his search wasn't over, just yet.

He found what was left of them – or most of them – in an encampment further on. The one who looked like Professor Foxx was not among them.

They were all wounded. Their wounds had been haphazardly bandaged, and they stank. They were dying from infection. Troy wondered if they knew that.

They turned to look at him without much interest when he walked into their camp. The embers of a fire glowed in a pit.

Troy saw his backpacker guitar beside one of them and picked it up.

"You mind?" he asked, politely, but did not wait for an answer as he examined the instrument. "This is a really nice guitar. I had one just like it. Hey, you know that song, 'Froggie Went a-Courtin'?' Springsteen does it on the *Seeger*

Sessions album? No? I'm sure you'd recognize it."

Troy played the guitar and sang the first verse.

Froggie went a-courtin' and he did ride, uh-huh
Froggie went a-courtin' and he did ride, uh-huh
Froggie went a-courtin' and he did ride
A sword and pistol by his side, uh-huh. Uh-huh. Uh-huh.

Troy let the chord ring out, feeling the weight of the cut-down in the scabbard at his side. He gently strummed the strings of the backpacker.

The wounded men eyed him warily. One of them had a pistol on the ground by his side, but Troy wondered if he had the strength to pick it up.

"Doesn't ring a bell, huh?" Troy said. "How about this version. Dan Zanes sings it. You know Dan Zanes? You have kids? Or had them? You know . . . *before*? No? Anyway, it goes like this:"

Froggie went a courting and he did ride
King kong kitchie kitchie ki-me-o
With a sword and a pistol by his side
King kong kitchie kitchie ki-me-o

Ki-mo-ke-mo ki-mo-ke
Way down yonder in a hollow tree
An owl and a bat and a bumble bee
King kong kitchie kitchie ki-me-o

Troy sang the entire song, all the verses, which, as with many of these old-time songs, were plentiful.

The men in the encampment listened, watchfully. Troy finished the song and smiled widely. "Isn't that a great song? I love your axe, man. It feels just like the one I used to have. Is it a Martin?" He looked at the brand. "Yeah, it's a Martin. I wanted to write 'This Machine Kills Fascists' on mine, you know, which is what Woody Guthrie wrote on his guitar. But then, I thought that might make it difficult, you know, to get on airplanes and such – not that that's an issue now, but it was then -- so instead my girlfriend wrote the phrase Pete Seeger used to have on his banjo: 'This Machine Surrounds Hate and Forces It To Surrender.' That's a beautiful idea, isn't it? Surrounding hate and forcing it to surrender. I love that. I wrote it write here." Troy pointed to the front of the backpacker. "Hey. Look at that. This one has that phrase written on it, too. Right here. Exactly the same place as mine. How about that? It looks just like my girlfriend's handwriting, too." He looked up from his guitar to the men staring back at him. "What are the chances?"

If they hadn't known before, the men knew now. The question was, what were they going to do about it?

They looked at Troy and Troy realized they'd given up the ghost, most of them.

He decided to provide them with an assist. He slung the backpacker over his shoulder and pulled the cut-down from the scabbard, racking a shell into the chamber.

Chapter Fifty-Seven

Mayor Dorothea Billings careened into Harper's office in something of a tizzy, which was becoming something of a regular occurrence.

"Harper," she cried, "how long do you intend to keep Henry locked in a cell?"

"Hello, Madame Mayor," Harper said, offering her a chair. "To answer your question, until the Magistrate sets bail or orders him released."

Mayor Billings sat down and slumped in her chair. "This could tear the valley apart."

Harper came around her desk and sat in the chair beside the Mayor. "Dory, you know we couldn't give into Lowry's demands."

"Couldn't we have negotiated? Did we have to shoot up the place?"

"We hardly shot up the place."

"The Council is not happy about this."

"What does the Council want me to do?"

"Make this go away."

"That's unlikely to happen at this point, Dory."

Dorothea sat regarding her fingernails for several moments. "How can we limit the fallout from this?"

Harper pulled her chair up closer to Dorothea. She could see the worry lines that seemed to have grown deeper on Dory's face. She wondered if the same was true of her.

"We need to treat Lowry like anyone else," Harper said.

"He can't be above the law."

Dorothea looked up at Harper, her eyes filled with worry. "Do you honestly think that's true?"

Chapter Fifty-Eight

Kim and Ingrid trudged to the house, hot and dirty after a long, hot morning working in the fields. Kim carried a shotgun and a pistol at her side. Ingrid carried the vintage Winchester. Once they reached the shade of the oak tree in the backyard, they took off their wide-brimmed hats. Ingrid went to the trough and pumped water, putting her face in the flow and gulping.

"It's your turn to make lunch," Kim reminded her.

"Fuck you," Ingrid said. "It's yours. I'm taking a shower."

"Don't take a shower."

"I'm stinky."

"It's only lunchtime. The workday is only half over. You're just going to get stinky again."

"Then I'll take another shower."

"That's so wasteful."

"Your ass is so wasteful."

"Yours is!"

"We recycle our water!"

"We recycle *most* of our water," Kim said, as patiently as possible. "Water is a finite resource. Like fuel."

"We need to take a siesta like they do in civilized countries," Ingrid said.

"There are no civilized countries anymore," Kim reminded her. "We're pretty much it."

"All the more reason to reinstitute the tradition of the siesta," Ingrid insisted. "When it gets too hot to work, we come in, eat, shower, nap, then go out again when the sun is not so hot."

"The sun is always hot. Even when the sun isn't hot, the air is."

Ingrid had had enough of her sister's relentlessly negative logic. "You're impossible."

"If you want to cool off, use the pump," Kim said, gesturing to the water trough and the old-fashioned cast-iron pump. "That's what it's for."

"You want me to stand at the pump and pour cold water on myself like I'm some kind of 19th century peasant?" Ingrid cried.

"Not like a peasant," Kim assured her. "Like a cowgirl."

Ingrid was not mollified. "Cowgirls smell like horseshit."

Now it was Kim's turn to reach her limit. "Oh, Jesus," she grumbled.

"I can't stand the smell of myself!" Ingrid exclaimed. "I smell like a smelly sweaty person! I don't want to be that person!"

"What person?"

"The smelly sweaty person!"

"Which smelly sweaty person?"

"Me! I smell like a cowgirl!"

Kim decided to attempt some redirection. "It's your turn to make lunch."

"You want a smelly sweaty cowgirl making your lunch?"

"Don't take a shower," Kim commanded.

"I'll make lunch after I take a shower!"

"You're impossible."

"Your ass is impossible," Ingrid countered, farted, and marched inside.

Kim stood alone and sulked.

Her sister was impossible. Her sister was a spoiled brat. Her sister farted too much.

Kim looked at the trough and the water glimmering. She felt the moisture of her perspiration on her skin and her smell rise from her sodden clothes.

Kim wanted a shower so badly. She knew her sister was only expressing what she also felt. But that was the difference between them. Just because you wanted something didn't mean you had to have it, or should.

Kim looked around. It was hazy, but she could see for miles around and saw not a soul.

She rested her shotgun on the picnic table and pulled her shirt from her chest. It was matted to her skin like glue. The stink of perspiration and heat wafted up.

Kim stripped naked and lay her clothes out on the railing of the gallery in the hopes they might dry before it was time to go back into the fields. She didn't want to have to put on fresh clothes – that was wasteful. Detergent was a finite resource. Still, she knew her sister had a point on this issue – their clothes were pretty unbearable to wear by mid-day, soaked through with perspiration, which risked chafing.

Her clothes laid out, Kim went to the trough, pumped fresh water into the pitcher, and poured it over herself.

The water was so cold, it took her breath away. It also felt better than anything had felt in a long time.

"That water looks refreshing," said a male voice she did not recognize.

Kim wiped water from her eyes and opened them.

A man stood there. He was bearded, in his fifties, she guessed. One arm was wrapped in a bloody bandage and hung in a sling.

In the other arm, he carried a rifle.

He also wore a torn and ragged t-shirt with a photograph of Johnny Cash flipping the bird to the camera.

Chapter Fifty-Nine

"Please pardon the intrusion," the man said. He was well-spoken, but Kim doubted his sincerity. She cursed herself for not noticing him when she'd scanned the surroundings. She wondered if he'd already been hidden and watching. Her heart was racing.

"I've just been walking a long way and I was wondering if I could trouble you for a drink of water?" the man said.

Kim looked towards her shotgun and wondered how quickly she could reach it.

"Now, that's interesting," the man said. "The first thing you do is look to your scatter gun. And not that water." He swung the rifle off his shoulder and pointed it at her casually. "I'll have that drink now, if it's not too much trouble."

He had made no comment on her nakedness. He looked at her thoroughly, but not lasciviously. Perhaps he didn't think anything of it. Perhaps post-apocalypse, old rules did not apply.

Kim was uncomfortable in her nakedness in front of this stranger, but less uncomfortable than she was about the rifle the man carried.

Kim went to the trough and pumped some water into a cup she kept nearby for that purpose.

"It'd be really kind if you could bring that to me," the man said. "You might have noticed, I've only got the use of one of my arms."

"Yeah, I'm pretty observant that way," Kim said, and

went to him, holding out the cup for him to take.

The man looked at the cup and then looked at her.

"If I take my good hand off of this rifle to take that cup, what do you think is going to happen?"

"I don't know," Kim said, thoughtfully. "What do *you* think is going to happen?"

"I think I don't want to find out. Can I ask you to put the cup to my mouth?"

Kim hesitated, then put the cup to the man's mouth. He drank, keeping his grip on his rifle the whole time.

"That's the sweetest water I've tasted in a long time," the man said. "How's your aquifer?"

"How do you know we've got an aquifer?"

"I can see your well. How's the water table?"

"Not as high as it used to be."

"Ain't that the truth?"

Standing close to him, Kim could smell the gangrene. "Your wound is infected," she told him.

The man cocked an eyebrow. "How do you know?"

"I can smell it."

"I apologize for that."

"Your blood is going to get infected if you don't have that taken care of."

"I'm aware," the man said.

"Do you want me to look at it?"

The man hesitated, considering. "Why don't we get to know each other a little better, first? I'm Foxx. With two X's. I used to be a professor."

Oh, shit, Kim thought.

"Really?" Kim said. It was her turn to cock an eyebrow. "I figured most intellectuals would have been dead by now. What are you a professor of?"

"Musicology."

Jesus Christ, Kim thought. This guy was Troy's professor. She didn't want to let on that she knew who he was, however. That struck her as imprudent. "You finding musicology to be a useful profession these days?" she asked.

"Well, it gives me a head full of songs to sing to myself when all around is bleakness and despair," Foxx said.

Kim shrugged. "I can see how that could come in handy."

"What do you do to take your mind off things?"

The tone was not exactly suggestive, but it unnerved Kim, nonetheless. "I don't take my mind off of things," she said.

The man grinned, slightly. Kim didn't like that grin. It felt knowing in a way she thought put her at a disadvantage.

"Never?" Foxx said.

"Sometimes when I go to sleep. If I'm lucky enough not to dream."

Foxx nodded to the house. "Nice place. You all alone out here?"

"Yes," Kim blurted out, and then immediately regretted her answer. What if he'd been spying on her and Ingrid?

Foxx narrowed his eyes. "You wouldn't lie to me, would you?" he said.

"No," Kim lied.

"If we go into your house, am I going to find any unpleasant surprises?"

"Who says you're going into my house?" Kim asked.

Foxx smiled. "I'm expecting you to invite me in, soon enough."

"Can I put my clothes back on?" Kim asked.

Foxx seemed to consider the question. "Not just yet, I don't think so."

Kim wasn't embarrassed by her nakedness, but she was afraid. She was both naked and afraid, she thought, and laughed to herself, bitterly.

"What's so funny?" Foxx asked.

"How did you get here?" Kim demanded.

"I'm asking the questions, I think."

Kim persisted. "How did you get here?"

"The guy with the gun gets to ask the questions."

"You didn't take the road into the valley, I know that,

because it's blocked."

"How do you know I'm not from the valley?"

"You're not from the valley."

"You know everyone in the valley?"

"Most everyone, yeah, and none of them are college professors. Did you hike over the mountain? Which trail did you use?"

"You ask a lot of questions for a girl without a gun."

"I have a gun," Kim reminded him. "It's over there." She pointed to her shotgun by the picnic table. "Why were you avoiding the main road?"

"Maybe you better get me another drink of water."

Kim got him another cup of water while Foxx sang:

"Get alone home Cindy, Cindy
Get a long home.
Get along home Cindy, Cindy
I'll marry you some day."

Despite the heat, Kim felt her blood run cold.

"Your name wouldn't happen to be Cindy, would it?" the man asked.

Kim went to him and put the cup to his lips. "My daddy used to sing that song," she said.

"I wrote a dissertation on it. It has a long, storied history, and multiple regional variations. But, of course, everybody loves the Dean Martin/Ricky Nelson duet the best."

"Rio Bravo," Kim said.

"That's right. I may be the only college professor in the valley, but I bet I'm not the only person around here with a college education."

"Elvis sings it too. Johnny Cash and Nick Cave as well."

"I could get used to talking to a girl like you."

"Well, don't get too used to it," Kim warned him.

"Why? You don't think I'm sticking around?"

Kim gritted her teeth. "Are you?"

"I think I might," Foxx said, looking at her in a way that

made Kim feel really naked for the first time since he'd arrived. "This isn't the first time we've been through this, you know." His tone had changed. He sounded . . . *professorial*, Kim thought. "This isn't the first time humanity has been through a near-extinction event. Seventy-five thousand years ago there was a massive die-off. Same reason as now. Scarcity of resources. We were reduced to just a few thousand of us. We bounced back that time. We'll bounce back this time. It's just a question of allocating resources. And maintaining a stable population that can be sustained by the resources available. We ran out of the necessary resources to sustain our population as it was. It's only natural we should experience another die off until we reach a sustainable level." He paused and looked around quickly. "This is by far the nicest place I've been in some time. Why don't you show me the interior?"

Kim had no intention of showing him the interior of anything, but wasn't quite sure how to phrase that.

Just then, Ingrid emerged from the house, showered, fresh, naked, and carrying a platter of sandwiches in one hand and the Winchester in the other.

"Lunch is served!" she announced, before she noticed Foxx.

Chapter Sixty

Ingrid and Foxx eyed each other warily.

"I thought you said no surprises," Foxx said.

"I said no *unpleasant* surprises," Kim said.

"Fair enough," Foxx conceded. "But I thought you said you live alone."

"How do you know she lives here?" Kim asked.

"She certainly seems at home."

"I meant *we* live alone."

"You weren't clear about that."

"You were pointing a gun at me," Kim said. "That always throws off my syntax."

"Why don't you introduce me?" Foxx suggested.

"I'm Ingrid," Ingrid said. She eyed him, warily. "Nice t-shirt you got there."

"Thanks," Foxx said. "That a real vintage Winchester?"

"I knew a guy named Troy had one just like it," Ingrid said. "The t-shirt, not the Winchester. He was traveling with a girl. She wore some kind of pendant. One day some guys pulled up in a pick-up and the next thing, he woke without the shirt or the girl. Or his pants for that matter."

There was a moment of stillness, and then things happened fast.

Ingrid dropped the platter of sandwiches. The platter clattered on the gallery floor, and the sandwiches bounced and came apart, scattering cheese and meat in all directions.

Foxx swung his rifle in Ingrid's direction.

Ingrid raised the Winchester and pumped the lever.

Kim dove to the ground.

Kim heard the loud report of a rifle shot, even louder than the thumping in her chest.

Foxx said, "Shit."

Kim looked up to see Foxx stumble and try to stay on his feet. There was blood seeping through his t-shirt, spreading over Johnny Cash.

Foxx tried to raise his rifle, but didn't seem to have the strength.

Ingrid pumped the Winchester and shot him again.

The bullet blew off Johnny Cash's middle finger and red gushed from the hole.

Foxx lurched back with the force of the bullet smashing into his chest, stumbled forward, and tried to stay on his feet.

The rifle dropped from his grip and then he fell to his knees.

Kim watched in awe as her sister marched to Foxx with long, powerful strides, pumping the Winchester again as she went.

"Did you see Troy again?" Ingrid demanded.

"That rifle got awfully heavy there," Foxx said, wheezing. "I think you shot through a lung."

"Troy," Ingrid said. "Did you see him again, since that first time?"

"I'm going to require medical attention," Foxx said. "Do you have that in this valley?"

"Listen to me," Ingrid said with a badass-itude Kim had never heard from her before. "Troy. He was with a girl. You and your goons stopped him and took his shirt and his girl."

After a moment, Foxx said, "He was in my Musicology 101 lecture course two years ago. He's an uninspired student. Not really intuitively musical. I recognized him. I felt bad taking his things and his girl. But what else was I supposed to do under the circumstances? Is he still alive?"

"What about his girl?" Ingrid pressed. "What did you do with her?"

Foxx hesitated. "I don't think you really want to know," he said, and coughed and sputtered. Blood sprayed from his mouth in a fine mist. "Can you see about getting me that medical attention now?"

Ingrid pressed the barrel of the Winchester to his forehead and pulled the trigger, blowing blood, brain, and bone out the back of his skull. Kim gasped. Foxx's body collapsed in a heap.

Kim stood there for a moment, not knowing exactly how to process all of this. "I didn't know you actually knew how to use the Winchester that well," she mumbled.

"I paid attention," Ingrid said. "You're a good teacher."

"Did you have to use so many bullets, though?" Kim asked. "Three bullets to kill one guy?"

Ingrid looked at her, enraged. "Seriously?"

"Bullets are a finite resource," Kim pointed out.

Ingrid glared at her, and farted.

Kim looked her over. She pointed at Ingrid's belly, which looked rounder and fuller than before. "I think you're starting to show," she said. "You'd better tell Harper, soon."

Ingrid was not mollified. "I am so not making you lunch again," she said.

Chapter Sixty-One

Percy and Harper stood outside the Sheriff's office. Most of her deputies were either still recovering from their wounds, manning the checkpoints, or guarding the pumping station by the reservoir.

The two stood facing a dozen armed men standing in the street facing them. Shopkeepers and passersby stood and watched the unfolding scene with alarm.

"What can I do for you gentlemen?" Harper said.

One of the men, a fellow named Trubo, Harper remembered, stepped forward.

"You need to release Mr. Lowry, now," Trubo said. He was tall, mustachioed, muscular, and thick around the middle.

Trubo seemed to be their leader, in Lowry's absence. If shooting started, she made a mental note to herself, she'd need to take him out first.

"When your boss is arraigned, the Magistrate will decide whether he gets bail or not," Harper said.

Trubo just stared at her. The men shifted restlessly. Harper didn't like the energy she felt in the air.

"Percy," she whispered. "Go inside and unlock the gun cabinet."

As Percy turned to go inside, Trubo shot him.

Percy collapsed against the door as Harper dropped to a knee and shot Trubo through the mouth. The bullet knocked out his teeth and burst out the back of his skull, spraying the men around him with blood and brain matter.

As she had anticipated, when she took out their leader, the rest of the men hesitated.

It was enough.

She dragged Percy through the door and bolted it behind her.

"I'm alright," Percy gurgled. Harper could tell he wasn't. He was pale and bleeding. Harper propped him against a wall, unlocked the cabinet, took out an M-4, and went to a window.

Four of Lowry's men were approaching the door while the others hung back.

Harper broke the glass and fired a burst that knocked all four men off their feet. Two, she could see, were killed immediately. One lay on his back, moaning. The other began to crawl slowly back toward his comrades.

Harper grabbed the emergency medical kit, brought it to Percy, and patched him up as well as she could.

Then she went back to the window and fired another burst.

Glass shattered all around her as Lowry's men returned fire and Harper dropped below the window to take cover.

She looked over at the wall and Percy was gone.

"Percy?" she called.

"I'm back here," Percy called back, weakly, from the back room where they kept the jail cells.

"Percy, what are you doing?"

"I've got my gun on Lowry, Sheriff," Percy said. "If those men come through the door, I'll put one through his brain pan."

"Sheriff," Lowry said. "My men will come through that door one way or the other. Your deputy looks pretty bad. I don't know if he's going to make it that long."

"You better pray I do, Mr. Lowry," Percy said, weakly but with conviction. "Because before I go, the last thing I'm going to do is empty my service revolver into you."

Harper thought perhaps she had underestimated her young deputy, as she rose and fired another burst through the shattered window.

Chapter Sixty-Two

They wrapped Foxx in an old sheet and put him in the meat locker.

"I don't want him in here next to Dad," Ingrid said.

The air cooled Kim's hair and flesh, which were soaked with sweat. She said, "We need to bury Dad."

"Oh, Jesus," Ingrid said. "Not this again."

"We can't keep him in the freezer forever. We need the space. We've got, like, the only working meat locker in the county. We can make much more productive use of it. Besides, it's gross to keep Daddy on ice next to our dinner."

Ingrid thought it over. "I think we should cremate him. Would we have to thaw him out first?"

"I'm not sure. It'll be hard to cremate him without a proper cremation furnace. We'd have to build a funeral pyre or something. And we'd have to get the fire to burn awful hot."

Ingrid smiled. "You can find a way," she said. "I have faith in you."

"We need to tell Harper about this," Kim said.

They left the meat locker, went indoors, and tried to reach Harper on the radio, but to no avail.

"I'll put on my sneakers, and walk into town," Ingrid volunteered.

"Take the Winchester," Kim said.

Chapter Sixty-Three

Ingrid walked into town, arriving hot and thirsty, and greeted by the sound of gunfire.

"What the hell is going on?" she asked Bart, who stood outside his saloon, the Silver Dollar.

"Lowry's men are trying to break him out of jail, I gather," Bart said. "I sure hope they don't hurt the Sheriff. I'd hate to lose her as a customer. There's no one else in the valley but her mom who makes so much honey, and her mom isn't much of a drinker." He glanced at her Winchester. "That thing shoot?"

Ingrid racked the lever. "I sure hope so," she said, and took off running.

When she arrived at the Sheriff's office, she saw five bodies lying in various positions on the steps leading into the entrance, or on the street in front of it. She counted seven men crouched across the street, firing rifles over the hoods of parked cars that hadn't moved since the gasoline ran out for everything but emergency vehicles, behind which they were taking shelter.

She heard a burst from the Sheriff's office, and turned to see Harper in the window, firing. The men in the street returned fire and Harper disappeared, the wood around the window splintering as bullets crashed into it.

Ingrid felt her heart sink and before she knew what she as doing, she strode along the sidewalk, the Winchester at her shoulder, and shot the man closest to her, crouching behind an old, green Dodge station wagon. The bullet went through his head and out the other side, splattering the green paint job with red. Ingrid racked the lever and strode on.

Amidst all the noise from the shooting, the other men didn't even notice what Ingrid had done. She strode on and came up behind a man with a graying beard crouching behind a Ford Bronco, firing over the hood. She shot him in the back, and he collapsed without knowing she was there.

The next two men, crouched behind a Chevy Blazer, turned and faced her as she racked the lever. One, she could see, was wounded. The other raised his rifle, a Remington. Ingrid shot him through the throat. The man dropped his rifle and gripped his wound, gurgling. The man beside him fumbled for a pistol. Ingrid racked the lever and shot him in the face from four feet away.

The man's face collapsed in on itself. The man beside him, blood pouring through his fingers clutching his throat, tried to get to his feet. Ingrid racked the lever and shot him through his chest.

Glass shattered next to her as a car window exploded and Ingrid looked up to see a man running towards her, pumping a shotgun and firing. The door to the Chevy Blazer suddenly was pockmarked with double aught. Ingrid racked the lever, crouched on the sidewalk, put the Winchester to her shoulder, took aim along the sightlines, and squeezed off a round. The bullet struck the man in the center of his chest and knocked him off his feet.

Ingrid stood and found herself facing a pistol barrel about one inch from her nose.

She cursed herself that she hadn't racked the lever yet.

She found she wasn't afraid to die, but she didn't want the baby inside her to die as well. That thought made her angry. She was also upset she wouldn't know for sure if Harper was alright.

A pistol shot rang out and roared in her ears. The top of the man's head exploded, and he collapsed.

Harper was standing there, her pistol raised, a wisp of smoke escaping from the barrel.

"Gross," Ingrid said. "I think I've got brains in my hair."

Harper looked down at the body lying at their feet. "That was Ebert Rollings. Did you know him?"

"I've met him," Ingrid said. "I wouldn't say I knew him. Do I have his brains in my hair? Be honest with me."

They heard a shot from the Sheriff's office. Harper turned and ran towards the sound. Ingrid thought that seemed foolish – you should run away from shooting. Of course, she herself had just done the opposite. After a moment, she turned and ran as well, following Harper.

In the back room, Henry Lowry lay on the floor of his cell, gutshot, his hands grasping his belly. Percy lay against the wall, pale, the makeshift bandage around his torso soaked through with blood.

"Percy's word was good, it looks like," Harper said, her hand on his neck, checking for a pulse. "He missed the brain pan, but he shot Lowry before he died, alright."

Lowry groaned.

"Hi, Henry," Ingrid said. "You don't look so well."

"Help me," Lowry said.

Ingrid regarded him. "I think you're a goner, Henry," she said. "But I can put you out of your misery, if you like."

Ingrid racked the lever on the Winchester one last time.

Chapter Sixty-Four

Harper sat at her desk, the Mayor facing her, sitting across from her, holding her head in her hands.

Ingrid was back home. The bodies had been cleared and taken to the morgue. The Mayor was not happy.

"I think the Council should give Percy some kind of a posthumous commendation," Harper said. "And his family should get some kind of a pension."

Dorothea looked at her, incredulously.

"He was a stand-up kid," Harper said.

"Harper, do you have any idea what kind of trouble this shit show you have created is going to make for me?" the Mayor said.

"I didn't create this shit show," Harper said, calmly. "Lowry did."

"Your girlfriend murdered a baker's dozen men, including Lowry, who was both unarmed and your prisoner at the time."

Harper narrowed her eyes. "Ingrid didn't murder anyone. She came to the defense of the county Sheriff when I was faced with a deadly assault during the performance of my duties. And who says Ingrid is my girlfriend?"

Dorothea rolled her eyes. "Everybody in town knows."

Harper was perplexed. "How?"

The Mayor was getting impatient. "Are you going to arrest her?"

"For what?"

"For murdering Lowry."

Harper was getting angry. "Ingrid didn't murder Lowry. Percy shot Lowry in the lawful performance of his duties."

"Since when is shooting a prisoner considered lawful?"

"Since armed bands of paramilitary thugs laid siege to the Sheriff's department and shot a deputy in an effort to break out said prisoner."

"This isn't the Wild West!"

Harper narrowed her eyes. "It kinda is, actually," she said. "I mean, when you've got gangs of outlaws trying to raid the town, and paid regulators trying to break a dude out of jail."

Dorothea looked up at the ceiling in exasperation. "I said this kind of thing could tear this valley apart."

"No one liked Lowry."

"No one liked him," Dorothea said. "Except the people who did. Those are the ones I'm worried about."

Harper put her gun and badge on the desk. "If you want them, they're yours."

Dorothea looked at the gun and badge in horror. "God no. There's no one else I can get to do this job."

"There's of *plenty* people who want to do this job," Harper said.

Dorothea looked Harper in the eye. "There's no one else I can *trust* to do this job."

"Apparently you don't trust me all that much. What do you want me to do?"

"Arrest your girlfriend."

Harper pushed the gun and the badge closer to the Mayor. "You'd better take these, then."

"Harper," the Mayor said. "There's got to be rules. There's got to be rule of law. People can't shoot prisoners."

"I understand there's got to be rules," Harper said. "I spend every day trying to make sure there are rules. But we've also got to accept that things are different. Sometimes we have to do things a certain way because there's no other way to do things." Harper pointed towards the cells in the back of the building. "No one is ever going to try to break someone out of here again."

"Well, no one is going to try to break Lowry out of here again," Dorothea said. "That's for sure."

"People need to know I mean business."

"The end justifies the means?"

"More like, we don't bring a copy of *Robert's Rules of Order* to a gunfight," Harper said. "Look, why are most of the people in this valley still alive? Why are you still alive, Dory? Why did we have enough meds to treat you when you got sick in the last outbreak? Because we broke the law to make sure we had what we needed. Because we were smart enough to recognize there was no more law, and the only way to maintain civilization was to improvise when we had to. That's what we did with Lowry, too. So, yeah. We had to break the law in order to maintain the law. That's irony, but it's irony we have to learn to live with, because there's no law and order if we're all dead. You don't like it, you can look for someone else you trust to take my job. But you better hope they're willing to make the tough calls."

Harper pushed the badge and gun still closer to the Mayor.

The Mayor stood up without taking the badge and gun. "You figure it out, then, she said. "Just, please, please, please, prevent a civil war from breaking out."

Harper watched the Mayor leave, and wondered if Dorothea was just being a nervous nelly, or if she should be really worried.

It was almost midnight by the time Harper made it out to Kim and Ingrid's place. She found Ingrid alone in the living room, dancing naked to Hayes Carll singing "Drunken Poet's Dream."

Harper watched her, in silence. Ingrid looked a little rounder, she thought. A little fuller. Her butt was bigger. She'd put on a little weight. She even had a little bit of a curve to her belly. It looked good on her, Harper thought.

When she saw Harper standing there, staring at her appreciatively, Ingrid stopped momentarily and said, "why don't you get out of that uniform and join me?"

Harper couldn't think of a good reason not to, so she did.

Later, cuddled in bed together, post-coital, flesh to flesh, Ingrid said, "I need to tell you something."

"Ok," Harper said.

"I'm pregnant," Ingrid said.

"Oh," Harper said, surprised. She blinked, as if a flash bulb had gone off in front of her eyes. "How pregnant are you?"

"Definitely first trimester," Ingrid said. "But end of the first trimester. Or beginning of the second. Somewhere in there." Ingrid was having trouble reading Harper's reaction. She found this alarming. She frowned. "I'm not getting an abortion, if that's what you're thinking."

"That isn't what I was thinking," Harper reassured her.

"Can you even get those anymore? Abortions?"

Harper considered the question. "I don't know if Doc Wilson would perform one, but people have been getting abortions for millennia, so, yeah, I'm sure there's a way. I'm sure there's an old medicine woman in a hollow around here who knows a non-surgical procedure."

"Do you think it's safe?" Ingrid didn't want to get an abortion, but she figured it was better to be well-informed, regardless.

"As safe as giving birth is these days."

That didn't sound reassuring, Ingrid thought. "People are still having babies."

"Doc Wilson delivered one just the other day," Harper said, then hesitated. "There were complications."

Ingrid raised an eyebrow. "Oh?"

"The mother almost bled out. It was touch and go."

"Wow." Ingrid was floored. She'd never considered the possibility that childbirth could be dangerous to a young, healthy person like herself. How had the human raced survived before modern medicine if having babies was so hazardous?

"They pulled through, though," Harper said, trying to be reassuring. "Mother and child both resting comfortably."

She examined Ingrid's face, which was full of doubt. "So, you're not considering an abortion."

"Well, *now* I am," Ingrid admitted. "Should I be?"

"That's up to you."

"You don't think I'm cut out for parenthood," Ingrid said, resentfully.

"I didn't say that."

"But you think it."

"I think we're all having to step up to the plate to do things we aren't necessarily cut out for," Harper said. "Like you. Killing the shit out of those guys."

Ingrid smiled. "How do you know I wasn't cut out for that already?"

"Well, the apocalypse does have a tendency to bring out hidden talents," Harper admitted. "As does parenthood."

Ingrid seemed thoughtful for a while. Then she got out of bed and left the room.

Chapter Sixty-Five

After twenty minutes, Harper went after her. She found her soaking in a bath of hot soapy water.

"That is so decadent," Harper complained. "Most people in the valley would kill to have hot running water."

"Will you join me?" Ingrid asked.

The idea made Harper feel guilty. But not guilty enough.

Harper slid into the tub behind Ingrid and wrapped her arms around her. Ingrid gripped Harper's powerful arms and rested her head against her chest.

"I thought you were putting on a little weight," Harper said.

Ingrid seemed mortified. "You think I'm fat?"

"I think you're gorgeous. The weight looks great on you."

"Will you still love me when I'm a huge, pregnant cow?"

"Ingrid, you are going to be the super-cutest pregnant girl in the world when you get big."

"Well," Ingrid said. "The world's a lot smaller than it used to be."

Harper put her hands on Ingrid's belly. "But your tummy won't be."

"I want to keep the kid," Ingrid said. "I'm scared, but I want to."

Harper put her hands on Ingrid's belly. "Then you absolutely should."

"I mean, who knows when I'm going to get a chance to have a kid again?"

"There's plenty of red-blooded American males in the valley who would love a chance to leave a bun in your oven."

"Yeah, but, I mean, I don't want to go around doing that if – "Ingrid trailed off.

"If -- ?" Harper said.

"If you and I have, you know – "

"What?"

"A future?"

Harper squeezed her tightly, feeling her heart swell. "Is that what you want? A future?"

"Everybody wants a future. The whole reason we're still alive is because we didn't succumb to the whole end of the world thing and opted instead to have a future."

"But I mean, a future . . . *together?*"

"I'm not asking you for anything," Ingrid said, quickly. "To take responsibility for this kid or anything. Or help me raise it or anything."

Harper pressed. "But you want us to have a . . . a future?"

"Yeah," Ingrid said. "I do. I mean, I know we haven't been seeing each other for that long, so, I'm not actually asking for a lifetime commitment or anything. I mean, maybe one day. But, yeah. I do. If you do."

Harper took a deep breath. "I'd love to help raise this kid with you. And, you know. *Be* with you. Have a future with you.

"Really?" Ingrid said, brightly.

"And, I mean, I don't feel we have to, you know -- Hedge our bets or anything. I mean, I know it's early in the relationship, but, I mean, the time for taking it slow, I don't know if that makes sense anymore. I think if it feels right, we have to have the courage to commit to it."

"You mean . . . *lifetime commit* to it?" Ingrid asked slowly and carefully, not wanting there to be a room for misinterpretation.

"Well, I mean, it's not just *us* now, is it?" Harper said. "There's a kid involved. So, yeah. I think if we're going to make a commitment, we have to be in it for the long haul."

Ingrid considered for a moment. "Are you asking me to marry you?"

"Well – "Harper hesitated.

"Yes," Ingrid said.

"Yes?"

"Yes, I'll marry you."

Harper stammered. "I -- really?"

Ingrid turned around in the tub and kissed her. "Do we even have that anymore?" she asked. "Marriage equality? I mean, does the Constitution still apply?"

Harper put her hands on Ingrid's soapy rump and pulled her closer.

"I guess we make our own rules now," Harper said, and kissed her back.

Chapter Sixty-Six

It was two weeks later when Troy approached Ingrid and Kim's house. From far off, he saw smoke, and feared the worst.

When he arrived at the farmhouse, however, he didn't know what to think.

Out back, he saw Kim, standing by a fire pit, holding a coffee can in her hands. She was naked and covered in ash.

She hadn't noticed him yet. She was staring into the fire.

Troy wasn't sure what he should do – turn away or announce himself. He inched closer.

"Are you ok?" Troy asked as he neared her.

Kim turned and looked at him. She didn't seem embarrassed, but she appeared confused, as if it was taking her a moment to process what she was seeing.

"I'm sorry," Troy blurted out. "I'll go."

"No," Kim said. "Stay."

She made no attempt to hide her nakedness. Troy stood there, awkwardly, not knowing what he was supposed to do.

Kim went to him and embraced him.

"I am so glad you're still alive," she said. "I was sure you were dead. I am so, so glad you're not dead. Gladder than I even thought I would be. I thought you were gone for good."

Her hair smelled of fire. He felt the fine layer of ash on her bare back where his hands held her.

"I came back," Troy explained. "There was nothing to

look for anymore." Troy told her about finding Lilly's remains on the side of the road. "I only knew it was her because she was still wearing this," he said, and held up the shark-tooth pendant. "I gave this to her. Last year. For her birthday."

"I am so, so sorry, Troy," Kim said, her eyes welling with tears.

"I want you to have this," Troy said, offering her the pendant.

Kim pulled back. "Oh. Oh no. No, come on. I couldn't. It's not right."

"It is," Troy insisted. "Do you think it's nice?"

Kim looked at the shark-tooth and smiled, just a little. "Of course."

"I want someone to have it for whom it will bring joy."

Kim looked at the pendant for a moment longer. "Ok," she said. "Will you put it on for me?"

Troy gently wrapped the pendant's chain around her neck and fastened it. His fingers touched the soot on her skin at her bare shoulders, and he felt himself tingle.

Kim fingered the pendant that hung between her breasts. "Thank you," she said.

"Thank you," Troy said, softly.

After a moment, Kim seemed to snap to attention. "Oh. Um," she held out the coffee can. "This is my father. His ashes. I just burned my father to ashes. Then I crushed what was left of his bones into powder. It was, um, dirty work. I thought my skin would be easier to wash off than my clothes, so that's why . . . ." she gestured to her bare torso. Then she choked back a sob. "I'm sorry."

"Don't be sorry," Troy said, softly.

That seemed to be what Kim needed to hear. She began to weep intensely. Troy reached out to her and took her in his arms. She buried her face in his chest and wept great heaving sobs. Troy held her for a long time.

When the sobbing began to subside, Kim said into his chest," you stink."

"I know," Troy said. "There's no running water out there."

"It's Ok," she said, and kept her face buried in his chest for a while longer while Troy held her. "I like your smell, even when it's stinky."

Finally, she lifted her head and looked up into his eyes. Hers were red and her tears had made rivulets in the ash on her face. "Well. Whew," she said. "I needed that. Sorry about your shirt. I got it all wet and snotty."

"Stop saying you're sorry. Hold on a second."

Troy went into the house.

Chapter Sixty-Seven

"I spoke to the County Magistrate," Harper said.

They were staying over at Harper's place, at Harper's insistence. Ingrid had bitched and moaned all weekend at the lack of electricity and the lack of hot running water. Still, she marveled at the breakfast Harper made for her in an iron skillet over a pot-bellied wood stove.

"We still have one of those?" Ingrid said. "A County Magistrate?"

"We sure do," Harper said. "And she says she'll marry us."

"Really?" Ingrid squealed. "When?"

"When do you want?"

"Soon!" Ingrid exclaimed.

"Really?" Harper said, hoping against hope.

Ingrid frowned. "What do you mean, 'really?'

"I guess I keep expecting you to change your mind," Harper admitted.

"Oh, ye of little faith."

"So, you want to set a date?" She tried to contain the joy bubbling inside of her. She didn't want to scare Ingrid away by appearing over-eager.

"Absolutely!" Ingrid exclaimed. Then, a serious look came over her face and she appeared thoughtful. "Except, we should scatter Dad's ashes, first."

"Of course," Harper agreed.

"And, I guess, wait a respectable time."

"A month?"

"A week?"

"Really?"

"Dad would think it was stupid to wait a whole month," Ingrid said.

"A week it is, then."

They kissed, tasting of bacon grease and eggs.

"Where will we live?" Ingrid asked.

"I thought you could move into my place?" Harper suggested.

Ingrid frowned. "Won't Kim be lonely?"

"I think she'll adjust."

"Well, I'll still need to help out on the farm."

"Are you sure?" Harper said. "You're pregnant, after all."

Ingrid looked offended. "Pregnant pioneer women used to work in the fields all day, come home, give birth to a kid, make dinner, and then go back out to the fields again with the kid sucking on their boobs."

"But you hate working the fields," Harper pointed out, she thought sensibly.

Ingrid furrowed her brow and looked severe, which to Harper made her look unbearably cute. "I'm not a slacker. I've got responsibilities, you know. I take my responsibilities seriously."

"Of course you do," Harper said reassuringly.

Chapter Sixty-Eight

"I have to tell you something," Ingrid said, as they sat together later on the couch, Harper sipping coffee. "Something I've been thinking."

"Ok," Harper said, feeling a little trepidatious.

"Well, I mean, the stuff you did," Ingrid said. "Organizing everyone and everything. I think the valley would be all Mad Max now if you hadn't done that."

Harper shrugged. "The people in this valley aren't murderers and rapists."

"But I bet most of the people out there weren't, either," Ingrid said, gesturing expansively to indicate the world outside the valley. "But then everything collapsed, and people got desperate. And people were too desperate to realize if they banded together and helped each other, they could get through it. I mean, not all of them could get through it. Maybe not even most of them. But some of them could. A lot more than did. But they didn't know that. Because they had no one to show them that. But you showed *us* that. You showed the valley, that."

Harper thought that over, but Ingrid could see her eyes welling with tears. "The people," Harper said, her voice cracking. "Outside the valley. The big box stores and the pharmacies and gas stations and gun shops. I robbed those people of a lot of resources." She held up her hands and stared at them, a far-away look in her eyes. "I've got blood on my hands," she whispered.

And then, suddenly Harper was weeping.

Ingrid had never seen Harper weep. Harper had always seemed so strong.

Ingrid didn't know what to do.

Then she took Harper in her arms and held her, while Harper wept into her bosom.

She held her for a long time, stroking her hair. Harper's body heaved with sobbing.

Ingrid worried about Harper. Would she recover from this? Was this some kind of breakdown? Was she not as strong as Ingrid had thought?

But it also felt good, Ingrid thought, to be the strong one, for once. This was something she could do. If Harper, with all the responsibilities she bore, needed a shoulder to cry on, Ingrid could be that for her.

Eventually, Harper's weeping subsided.

Ingrid put her hands on Harpers shoulders and sat her upright. Then she put her hands on the sides of Harper's head and looked into her red and swollen eyes.

"Harper," Ingrid said. "We've all got blood on our hands." Ingrid kissed a tear from Harper's cheek. It tasted salty. "We all burned too much oil and sprayed our hair too much and consumed too many resources and exhausted this planet until there was almost nothing left and now almost everyone is dead." Ingrid kissed away a tear from another cheek. "We all did that. But you, Harper. I think, maybe, you rescued Western Civilization, if we're the last of it." Ingrid kissed a tear that hovered at the end of Harper's nose.

"I think that's a little much," Harper said wiping the remaining tears on her sleeve and trying to recover.

"Your ass is a little much."

Harper frowned. "You don't like my ass?"

"I love your ass. I'm just saying, is all."

"That my ass is a little too much?" Harper said. "My ass is too big?"

"That everyone alive in this valley thinks you're a superhero."

"Your ass thinks I'm a superhero."

"My ass included."

Ingrid kissed her, then told her to stand up and turn around.

"No," Harper demurred. "I'm shy."

"We need to cure you of that," Ingrid said.

Harper stood, and turned, her back to Ingrid. Ingrid reached around her, unbuckled Harper's pants, and pulled them down to her ankles.

"What are you doing?" Harper asked.

"Checking out that big ass of yours," Ingrid said. "Getting an idea of what mine is going to look like, soon enough."

"Hey," Harper said, and was quiet as Ingrid gently kissed one buttock, and then the other, as she slid her hand between Harper's thighs.

They made love on Harper's bed and after, Harper drifted off to sleep. She awoke to find Ingrid sitting beside her, flipping through the Polaroids Daryl had taken.

"Where did you find those?" Harper asked.

"In your bureau," Ingrid said.

"What were you doing rummaging in my bureau?"

"I didn't know it at the time, but looking for these, apparently," Ingrid said. She held up the pictures Daryl had taken while they made love, with Harper facing both away and towards the camera. She pointed to Daryl's junk, visible in both shots as Harper straddled him. "This looks familiar, by the way," Ingrid said. "Do I know him?"

Harper was embarrassed, and also a little aroused by Ingrid's scrutiny of these pictures. She wondered if Ingrid had also made love to Daryl. He had a reputation as something of a playboy, so Harper thought it was certainly possible, maybe even probable. She wondered if Daryl was the father of Ingrid's baby. She decided she was glad that Daryl's face didn't appear in any of the Polaroids . . . even if his erection did. "Are you jealous?" Harper asked, playfully.

"Both turned-on and jealous," Ingrid admitted. She held up a picture of Harper posing naked but for her hat, gun-belt, and cow-boy boots. "Will you take some Polaroids of me in the same get-up?"

"Really?"

"We can have a matched set."

Harper smiled. "Ok," she said. "But I'm taking the clip out of my sidearm."

Chapter Sixty-Nine

Kim stood there, alone, in the yard, waiting for Troy to come back and suddenly felt kind of stupid standing there naked and covered in ash.

'Hey, you know, now that you're not dead and everything?" Kim called into the house, desperately trying to figure out what to say and do in this circumstance. "Ingrid says you have a pretty good singing voice. And, you know, you're a musicologist. So, you know, there's a lot of old timey music hidden away in the hollows around here. Stuff that's never been archived, and, you know, even if it has, I mean, the Library of Congress is probably just so much kindling now, you know? Or, probably underwater, actually, so all those books and recordings are, like, mush. And, like, I don't know. I don't know what, like, American culture is anymore, or what it's going to be. I mean, is there going to be an American culture? Or just a culture of, like, this valley? And there's probably, like, other pockets of life out there, but will we ever contact them? I mean, maybe we will, one day. After the road warriors die off, which they will probably do eventually, because, you know, no food and gasoline and stuff. So, maybe one day it'll be, like, safer to travel outside the valley. And then, like, well, maybe we'll get in touch with other communities. Although, by then, I mean the roads and the highways could be pretty much weeds. So, this might take a while. And by that time, who knows if we'll still be sharing the same culture? We could be, like, two different countries. Even our use of English could be so different that we won't understand each other.

So, I don't know whether you'd be preserving American culture, or just valley culture. But I'm thinking that whatever it is, it's a culture, and it's worth something, and it should be preserved. And maybe you and Ingrid can go around the valley and learn the songs and stories and stuff from the old timers who still remember them and, you know, keep the culture alive."

Troy emerged from the house with a basin of hot, soapy water and some washcloths. He put them down on the picnic table.

"Be still," he said, as he wet a cloth and wiped the soot, tears, and snot from Kim's face. Then he discarded the cloth, wet another, and began to wipe the soot from her shoulders.

"I don't know how much of this is wood ash," Kim said. "And how much of this is Daddy."

Troy continued to wash her shoulders, moving to her arms.

"Those men who tried to breach the checkpoint?" Troy said. "You guys don't have to worry about them anymore."

He was washing her back now. Kim felt the warm water run down the slope of her back and over her buttocks.

"You didn't strike me at first as a warrior type," Kim said.

"I'm definitely not a warrior type," Troy concurred. "But you showed me how to use the shotgun."

"You have to get in mighty close with a shotgun."

"They were all shot up already," Troy said. "Harper and her deputies did a number on them. And I took them by surprise. So, it was pretty easy. Rack, then *blam*. Repeat. A mopping up operation. That's what they call it in the comic books."

He ran the washcloth over her rump without hesitating. Kim felt herself tense a little bit at the intimacy, her buttocks clenching. She found herself hoping she didn't look stupid with her ass all clenched up like that.

"There's no one else out there," he continued. "I didn't see another living soul. Remember how I told you they stopped picking up the bodies in the city? I don't think they ever started to pick them up in these small towns. There were bodies in the streets. In the cars. In the houses."

"You really stink," Kim said. "Take off your clothes."

Dutifully, Troy put down the washcloth and stripped naked, laying his clothes out on the picnic table bench.

He turned to face her.

Kim picked up another washcloth, wet it, and put it gently to his face.

Troy took up his washcloth and put it again to hers.

In tandem, they wiped the ash and grime from one another. It came off in streaks.

"What about the farms?" Kim asked. "You must have found farms."

She moved to his shoulders and arms and neck, and he to hers.

"It was mostly big corporate farms, and most of them went belly up when the drought hit and the crops failed years ago. The ones that stuck it out, they all collapsed when the grid went down. They were just abandoned, overgrown, livestock left to die and rot in their pens, the manure pits left to fester in the sun. The stench was unbearable -- you could smell it for miles. The few smaller farms, they were destroyed, the houses burned, the crops dead. Sometimes there were corpses rotting away inside their clothes scattered around. I think the road warriors raided the farms for what they could get, never considering, you know, a farm is a long-term proposition. Something that could have sustained them. Sustained a community. But they didn't think of that. They weren't thinking about community. They just thought of what they wanted right now. Which was to steal food and rape girls. I guess the prospect of long-term agricultural development probably seemed pretty remote to them, given the conditions. And maybe they were right. Maybe it will be decades before anything can seriously grow out there again, if ever. The soil is parched, dust everywhere, the sun relentless, hardly any water. The upside of that is, eventually, the road warriors are going to die out, once they run out of gasoline to salvage and things to steal." Cautiously, he moved to her chest, running the cloth over her breasts. Kim gasped when he touched her there, felt her nipples harden, then put her cloth to his chest. "I found some clarity out there," Troy said.

"Please share," Kim asked. "I could use some clarity."

"I just figured that, instead of trying to hold onto the bits of our lives from before so that we can try to piece together some kind of a Xerox of a Xerox of a Xerox of the way things used to be, we have to start figuring out the way things actually are, now, and finding our way to making a life out of that."

"That makes sense," Kim said. "Especially since there are no Xerox machines anymore."

Kim held her breath as Troy gently lifted one breast, and then the other, to wipe down the area behind them. She tingled all over when he did so, her body shimmering with a sense of uncertain expectation. The intimacy of the gesture was exhilarating. He continued down her sternum, and Kim slowly let out her breath, which was by now bursting in her lungs.

They had reached one another's bellies, and moved further down to one another's thighs. They both hesitated, and then, as if in silent communication, they put the cloths to each other's genitals.

Kim felt everything inside her spark as her loins filled with heat and she felt Troy immediately become hard.

Kim cast aside the cloth and took him in her fist. Troy cast aside his, and put his fingers to her sex. Kim felt sensations pulsing inside her. They drew close, their flesh pressing into one another, and kissed.

He went down on her without prompting, gripping her buttocks in his hands as he put his mouth between her thighs. He brought her to climax with finesse and passion.

As her ardor ebbed, he rose, and they kissed, then Kim dropped to her knees and took him in her mouth. He came almost immediately.

He helped her to his feet and he initiated the kiss, kissing her hard without hesitation, the tastes of their fluids mingling on their tongues. Her hands groped his skinny body and she felt him get hard again.

He hoisted her off her feet then and gently put her down at the edge of the picnic table and Kim, only a little concerned about getting splinters in her ass, opened herself to him as he positioned himself and entered her.

"I have your t-shirt, by the way," Kim gasped breathlessly, her fingers comfortably intertwined with the greasy locks of his hair, as she felt him thrust deep inside her. "The one of Johnny Cash flipping the bird. It's drying on the line." She shuddered, as she repeatedly came with increasing intensity in concert with his thrusts. "It's got a couple of holes in it."

Chapter Seventy

It was a few weeks later as the four of them were setting the table for dinner that the rock came through the window.

They all paused what they were doing and looked towards the broken glass on the hard wood floor. They could hear wind and the murmur of voices beneath it from outside.

"That can't be good," Ingrid said.

Harper moved towards the front door, grabbing her pistol belt as she went.

Kim stepped in front of her. "I'll handle this," she said.

"Do they have pitchforks and torches?" Ingrid asked. "I always knew our jealous neighbors would show up with pitchforks and torches one day."

"Shut up," Kim said, and stepped outside.

The small crowd did not have torches or pitchforks. A few, however, carried shotguns. Kim took some small comfort than none of the shotguns were pointed directly at her.

She recognized some of Lowry's few surviving men, which didn't surprise her so much. It was the other people she worried about. They were friends and neighbors. Well, neighbors, anyway. She doubted many of them could be counted as friends. Most had come on foot. She noticed a few horses and one mule at the edge of the crowd.

"Y'all want some cold beer?" Kim said. "You know my daddy taught us to make our own. I still think we got about a hundred bottles on ice, that'll be, I'm guessing, two and a half per person."

She waited for an answer. None was forthcoming.

"We ain't here for your beer, Kim," said Scotty Hubbard, finally. He'd taken her to prom once upon a time, seemed like a million years ago. They'd lost their virginity together in the back seat of his rusty old Jeep Wrangler. She hadn't seen much of him after she went off to college.

"What *are* you here for, Scotty?" Kim asked.

Scotty shuffled his feet uncomfortably and looked at the ground.

"We're here for your sister, Kim," Lacey Rollings said. Kim recognized her. She was married to one of Lowry's men. Kim wondered if her husband had been one of the men killed during the attempted jailbreak. She was about thirty-five, and she looked angry.

Kim screwed up her face. "What on earth do you want my sister for?"

"She killed Lowry," said a grumpy-looking fat man with a shotgun. Kim recognized him but couldn't remember his name.

"Y'all hated Lowry," Kim said. "Everybody did."

"Well, that's not exactly the point, Kim," Scotty Hubbard said.

"What is the point, Scotty?" Kim asked.

Scotty looked sheepish and suddenly unsure of himself.

"There's got to be justice," Lacey said.

"Lowry got what he deserved," Kim said. "Most people I know would call that justice."

"Did Ebert get what he deserved?" Lacey cried. "Did my husband get what he deserved?"

So, Kim's suspicion had been correct. "Did Ebert die trying to break Lowry out of jail?" Kim asked.

Lacey looked down at her feet.

"I'm sorry that happened, Lacey," Kim said. "But you know as well as I do why it happened." Kim looked at the crowd. "You all know why Ebert died," she said. "And you all know why Lowry did, too."

Lacey looked up, her eyes brimming with tears, and

spittle flew from her mouth as she shouted, "I can't get your sister for what she done to Ebert, 'cause they're calling that self-defense. But we can for what she done to Lowry, 'cause that was plain murder."

Kim could hear the front door open and then Harper was beside her, her gun belt on, her hand resting on the butt of her pistol.

"I said I would handle it," Kim whispered.

"This isn't about you," Harper said.

"I know it isn't about me, it's about my sister," Kim said.

"It isn't about her, either."

"Ingrid isn't going to come out here with the Winchester, is she?"

"I certainly hope not," Harper said. Then she took a step toward the crowd. "Y'all have concerns about what happened in the jail, you bring them up with me. I was in charge and everything done was done under my authority."

"You're just protecting your girlfriend!" Lacey shouted.

"Lacey," Harper said, regretfully. "Ingrid didn't kill Ebert. I did. I did, and I'm sorry I had to, but I'm not sorry I did. I'd do it again. Ebert left me no choice."

Lacey opened her mouth to say something, but the words stuck in her throat. She stood there as tears began to run down her face.

Some in the crowd were looking at each other, uncomfortably, Kim thought. They looked embarrassed, and like they had suddenly discovered a bad taste in their mouths. Kim saw Scotty pull aside some men and speak to them, a look of concern on his face. Maybe, just maybe, she thought, they were trying to find a way to back out of this.

Just then the front lawn was flooded with flashing blue lights. A Crown Vic came over the hill in the road and pulled into the driveway and up to the crowd.

Deputy Dawkins climbed out, painfully, his arm still in a sling. He was followed by the Mayor, Daryl and . . . Raymond Tilly Junior, all of ten years old.

"What's going on here?" Dorothea asked.

"This don't concern you, Mayor," Lacey said.

"Oh, I think it does, being Mayor and all," Dorothea said.

Daryl grinned one of his super-sexy grins at Harper and Kim. "How you girls doing?" he said.

OhMyGod, Kim thought. Harper slept with him, too, she realized. She could tell by the way he looked at her.

Raymond Tilly Junior climbed up the front porch stairs and stood by Harper. "What's wrong with y'all?" Raymond Junior said. "Don't y'all know the Sheriff saved each and every one of you a dozen times over?"

"You get on back to the trailer trash in Melzingah Hollow," said the fat man with the shotgun.

"Hey," Daryl said. He looked angry. He walked up to the man. "You say something mean to the kid again, and I'm gonna knock you on your ass."

The man looked at Daryl. The shotgun shifted in his grip.

Daryl snatched the shotgun from the fat man's hands and hit him in the face, knocking him on his ass. The fat man sat there, holding his bleeding nose.

"Alright," Scotty said. "This was a mistake. Let's all go home."

But Lacey would not be moved. "Why you protecting that rich bitch?" she shouted to Harper, through sobs. "Her snatch taste that good?"

The crowd hushed, stunned into silence. Even Lacey stopped her sobbing.

Harper stared at Lacey. "It does, actually," she said.

Kim wouldn't have thought it possible, but the crowd grew even more silent.

Then Ingrid came from the side of the house. Kim was grateful she wasn't carrying the Winchester.

Instead she was carrying a tub of ice cream. She was followed by Troy, who carried another. Ingrid had her guitar slung on her back. Troy had his backpacker guitar slung on his.

Ingrid's baby bump was by now clearly showing, her mid-riff bare below her tank top.

"My snatch don't taste half as good as this tub of mint chocolate chip, though," Ingrid said, cheerfully. "Y'all want some ice cream?"

After Lacey and the Lowry crew sulked away along with the angry fat man, the rest of the crowd stayed and drank all of their beer and listened to Troy and Ingrid sing and play guitar while they ate most of their ice cream.

It was worth the sacrifice, though, Ingrid thought.

Kim handed Troy an armful of dirty spoons and bowls and sent him into the kitchen to start the dishes. Once he disappeared indoors, she turned to Harper and Ingrid.

"So," she said. "We all slept with Daryl and one point. Am I right?"

Harper looked like she'd been caught.

Ingrid gasped. "You slept with Daryl too?" she said to Harper. Then she gasped again. "That was his junk in those Polaroids!"

"Do I want to know what you're talking about?" Kim said, skeptically.

"I'm sure you don't," Harper said quietly, sending a warning look at Ingrid.

Ingrid was laughing.

"Daryl's the father of your baby, isn't he?" Harper said.

Ingrid stopped laughing. "I don't want him to know."

"Why not?"

"Because I want *us* to be the only parents to my baby," Ingrid said.

The embarrassment disappeared from Harper's face. She took Ingrid in her arms, and they kissed.

"Does my snatch really taste that good?" Ingrid asked, between kisses.

"Oh, good grief," Kim said.

"It does," Harper confirmed. "Every part of you tastes that good."

"Even better than Chunky-Monkey ice cream?" Ingrid asked.

"Oh, sweet Jesus," Kim said.

Harper slipped her hands down the back of Ingrid's

pants, taking hold of her rump. "Even better."

Ingrid beamed with delight. "You do, too. Every part of you tastes even better than Chunky-Monkey ice cream."

They began to make out with purpose, hands caressing up and down one another's torsos.

Quickly and quietly, Kim slipped inside to help Troy with the dishes.

Chapter Seventy-One

It was a week later, and Ingrid and Harper sat on the porch swing on the gallery, Ingrid holding her dad's ashes in the coffee can. They were both dressed in black.

What was that movie?" Ingrid asked.

"Which movie?" Harper said.

"The one with Jeff Bridges."

"*Crazy Heart.*"

"Not that one."

"*The Fabulous Baker Boys.*"

"No."

"*True Grit.*"

"No."

"*The Last Picture Show.*"

"No."

"*Eight Million Ways to Die.*"

"*Eight Million Ways to Die?*" Ingrid repeated, incredulous.

"With a young Andy Garcia as the bad guy," Harper explained.

"Not that one. How many Jeff Bridges movies have you seen?"

"All of them."

"Really?"

"I love Jeff Bridges," Harper said. "*Fisher King?*"

"No."

"*Thunderbolt and Lightfoot.*"

"No."

"Tron."

"No."

"Against All Odds."

"Oh!" Ingrid exclaimed. "I love that movie!"

"Is that the one?"

"No."

"Wild Bill."

"No."

"White Squall?" Harper suggested. *"Blown Away? The Mirror Has Two Faces? The Jagged Edge? Starman? Nadine? Tucker? The Morning After? King Kong?"*

"No."

"Arrghh!" Harper exclaimed in frustration. Then, a thought occurred to her. *"The Big Lebowski?"*

"That's the one!" Ingrid cried in delight.

"What about it?"

Ingrid held up the ashes. "Just like at the end of that movie, right? With the ashes in the coffee can."

Harper wasn't so sure. "I guess. But that was played for laughs."

"That's totally how we should play this, too," Ingrid said, then frowned. "I'm pissed at Kim for cremating Dad without me."

"Don't be pissed. You couldn't have handled it."

This made Ingrid mad, which Harper thought was cute. "Your ass couldn't have handled it."

"You know you would have hated every second of it."

"I'd have still liked to have been asked," Ingrid said.

Harper kissed her.

"What are you doing?" Ingrid said.

"You know what I'm doing," Harper said, and kissed her again.

"Why?" Ingrid said.

"Do I need a reason to kiss my fiancé?" Harper asked, still kissing her.

"But what have I done to deserve such affection?"

"Just being you is enough for me," Harper said, and this time, Ingrid kissed her back.

Chapter Seventy-Two

Kim and Troy emerged from the house dressed in funeral black and found Harper and Ingrid similarly attired, making out.

"Oh, gross," Kim said. "Knock it off, lovebirds. Get a room."

Ingrid waved at Troy. "Hi, Baxter," she said.

"Troy," Troy reminded her.

"If you insist," Ingrid said.

"Ok," Kim said, indicating the coffee can containing her father's ashes. "How do we do this?" She turned to Troy. "Dad didn't want a funeral. But I figured we should do something to mark his passing. You know. Closure and all that. Then we'll dump his ashes in the compost."

"Dad would have wanted it that way," Ingrid concurred, nodding.

"Remember that song, Ingrid?" Kim said. "The first one Dad taught you on guitar?"

"Oh! Yeah," Ingrid said, brightly. "I haven't played that one in forever." She picked up her guitar. "I think I remember it."

She began to strum the chords, then sang:

There's a dark and a troubled side of life;
There's a bright and a sunny side, too;
Tho' we meet with the darkness and strife,
The sunny side we also may view.

Keep on the sunny side, always on the sunny side,
Keep on the sunny side of life;
It will help us every day, it will brighten all the way,
If we keep on the sunny side of life.

Strumming the chord sequence, she turned to Troy. "Play with me, Baxter."

Troy ran inside, picked up his backpacker, returned, and began to play along. Ingrid sang another verse.

"Sing the chorus with me, you damn slackers," she cried, when the chorus came around.

Everyone joined in and sang with her:

Keep on the sunny side, always on the sunny side,
Keep on the sunny side of life;
It will help us every day, it will brighten all the way,
If we keep on the sunny side of life.

Ingrid finished, letting the final chord ring out.

Everyone stood in silence for a moment.

"That song was written in 1899," Troy said. "The Carter Family recorded it in 1928 and made it more famous. Oh, um. Hey, Ingrid?"

"Yes, Baxter?" Ingrid said, dreamily.

"I've been meaning to tell you -- thanks for protecting Kim. And, like, getting my t-shirt back and everything. When you killed the fuck out of that guy, Foxx, I mean. But, mostly, um. For Kim. And also for giving away all your ice cream to placate the angry mob and everything. Thanks for that. Too."

Ingrid smiled. It felt good to be acknowledged for doing something useful for once. "No problem, Troy. Any time."

Chapter Seventy-Three

In silence, they all trudged down to the compost. Ingrid and Kim opened the lid of the coffee can, and, together, each holding one side, upturned it and let the ashes fall in a cloud upon the compost.

They all stared at the ashes in a heap on the compost for a moment.

Ingrid was the first to hear it. She turned to the sky.

"Hey, look," she said, as droplets of water began to sprinkle, then pour from the dark clouds above them and onto their upturned faces.

Ingrid pulled the black dress over her head. She was not wearing underclothes. She stood there, naked, her arms raised to the sky, letting the rain fall on her skin. She looked spectacular, Kim thought, in her nakedness, standing in the rain with her upturned arms, her baby bump by now clearly showing.

The others exchanged glances. They were unsure how to proceed. Kim knew they were looking to her for a sign.

Kim shrugged. It was not the most ridiculous way to celebrate her father's legacy, she thought.

She nodded, and began to strip off her own clothes. Troy followed suit.

Disrobed, the three of them stood there, naked in the deluge.

Ingrid began dancing in the rain.

Kim laughed, and then she began dancing, too.

Troy looked at Harper, shyly. She stood there, not yet ready to embrace the nakedness and abandon. Then Troy too, awkwardly at first, but with increasing joyfulness, began to move and sway in rhythm to the beating raindrops.

Ingrid began to twirl and prance across the lawn, stopping to splash into puddles.

Kim and Troy followed, leaving their clothing lying there in sodden heaps.

Harper watched them, considering. Then, finally, she stripped naked as well and went to join them, taking a moment to collect her rifle and the Winchester, running to catch up.

When she reached them, Harper, to her own surprise, broke into an exuberant step-dance, her feet splashing wildly in a muddy pool.

They all danced together in the cooling, powerful rain, splashing in puddles with their feet, the slashing raindrops stinging their skin with their power, until the thunder got a little too close for comfort, and bolts of lightning began to split the sky.

They ran to the shelter of the gallery, where they continued dancing, hair and flesh dripping, to the rhythm of the raindrops as they crashed to the gallery's tin roof and rolled from the gutters to the thirsty earth.

Finally, spent, they all leaned on the gallery railing, looking out at the big, black clouds undulating in the sky across the valley, spitting out occasional bolts of electricity, leaving rolling rumbles of thunder in their wake that echoed between the mountains.

"Well, what do you know?" Harper said.

Kim, in a whisper, said, "Rain."

The End

ABOUT THE AUTHOR

Peter Ullian's publications include the *The Triumphant Return of Blackbird Flynt* and *Big Bossman,* both from Broadway Play Publishing; *New American Century & Fair City* and *Pan-American,* both from NoPassport Press; and *The Fevered Dream-Crimes of Pulp-Fiction Poets and Other Love Stories: New and Selected Poems* from Lion Autumn Music Publishing. He is the 2019-2020 Poet Laureate of the City of Beacon, New York.

www.ingramcontent.com/pod-product-compliance
Lightning Source LLC
Chambersburg PA
CBHW031631130726
47900CB00019B/2402